MW00974384

Untouched

Higher Elevation Series
Book Two

By Renee Regent

Jauanita,
Thanks for
every ming !
Enjoy !
Renee Regent

To join the author's mailing list visit http://reneeregent.com
Copyright © Renee Regent 2016
Edited by Lina Sacher
Cover design by Funky Book Designs

Royal Turtle Publishing
royalturtlepub@gmail.com

This is a work of fiction. Names, characters, places, and incidents are a product of the author's imagination or are used fictitiously. Any resemblance to actual events, locales, or persons, living or dead, are coincidental.

Untouched
Higher Elevation Series
Renee Regent
ISBN: 978-0-9981328-3-9

The author acknowledges the trademark status and trademark owners of various products or copyright material mentioned throughout this work of fiction, including the following: Atari, Gilligan's Island, Volkswagen Beetle, Volkswagen Mini Bus, Ford Pinto, Jet Ski, and Ouija Board Game. The publication and use of these trademarks is not authorized, associated with, or sponsored by the trademark owners.

Thanks to all my Atlanta writers for their support and feedback. Thanks to Lina Sacher for her editing expertise, and Suzanna Lyons of Funky Book Designs for her awesome cover work. Special Thanks to Joe Green for the Colorado memories.

Table of Contents

1 Friends

Fort Winston, Colorado
Summer 1978

There had been a time in his life when Zac Daley loved surprises. Now, he hated them. Yet here he was on his way to see the girl he'd been trying to forget, the one who just wouldn't take no for an answer. Amanda Bresky was a force to be reckoned with, and today she had a big surprise for him.

Granted, it was his birthday, but to him it was just another day in the middle of June. His only plan for celebration was to go out with a few of the guys after work, grab a steak and a beer or two. But Amanda had called and against his better judgment, he agreed to meet her.

He turned his beat-up '68 Volkswagen Beetle onto Buckhorn, the winding road which lead to Horse Tail Reservoir Recreation Area. They were meeting at noon at the picnic pavilion, which overlooked the lake below. It was shaping up to be another gorgeous Colorado day with not a cloud in the sky, but he knew from experience that could change in a hurry. As he climbed the hill with his car windows open, he realized his long, bushy hair would be a mess, but it was too damned nice out to worry about it. Amanda wouldn't care anyway.

It was a short walk from the parking area to the pavilion, which was already filling in with families hauling coolers full of food. The aroma of burgers searing on a grill made his stomach growl, and he hoped this surprise of hers included some type of sustenance because he was starving. He spotted her easily—her red hair was hard to miss in a crowd. He made his way to her, his heart beating louder than he knew it should be.

She deserves better than I can give her. Why won't she just accept it?

Emotions that had laid untouched in his soul, just where he wanted them, threatened to resurface every time he was in her presence. His red-headed tormentor looked up and saw his approach, her eyes sparkling.

She really liked him, almost idolized him, and he had no idea why.

"Zac, over here!"

She waved and ran to him, clasping him in a hug. He held her for a moment, taking in her perfume, some exotic floral scent he couldn't name. She released him and took his hand, leading him to a picnic table at the edge of the pavilion.

"I hope you're hungry. I made us lunch."

"I'm famished, but you didn't have to do all this, Amanda."

She turned to him, her dark copper eyes flashing. "I wanted to. I've missed you, and it's your birthday."

The table was covered with a red checkered cloth and laden with food, more than the two of them could possibly eat. He looked around, wondering if this was a surprise party, but to his relief he didn't recognize any of the other people milling around the tables. She told him to sit and handed him a soda, his favorite—root beer. Then she handed him a plate of ham, potato salad, baked beans, and another favorite, pierogis.

"My Mom will kill me if she finds out I took those, but I know how you love them," she confessed. "And look, I even made a cake."

She had—chocolate with cream cheese icing, and covered with pecans. She was using everything in her arsenal this time, and it almost made him laugh.

"You are freaking amazing, Miss Bresky. You know that?"

"I try."

"Thanks. I don't know what to say."

"Just eat."

He had to admit, it was the best meal he'd had in a while. In the few weeks since his graduation from Fort Winston University, he'd moved out of the dorm and into a furnished studio apartment where he could pay by the week. It had a tiny kitchen, but he wasn't much of a cook anyway. He hadn't even bought dishes yet, since he didn't know how long he was going to stay in Colorado.

The fact was, he should have left already; he should have planned his next step months ago. New Jersey was where he belonged, it was home. But he knew life there would never be the same as it was when he left. It had been four years and he knew he couldn't put off going back there forever. He'd have to face his family sometime, but for now, he just needed time to breathe. Time to decide what the hell he was going to do with his life.

Twenty minutes later, he was much more relaxed. Amanda chatted on, talking about her summer job at the library, and what her friends were up to. He watched her, fascinated by her natural beauty, her effervescent personality, and her obvious adoration for him. She was dressed in a brightly colored tee shirt and cut-off denim shorts, which showed off her long, tanned legs. An avid runner, she loved track at school, and her athletic grace showed in her deft movements as she packed up what was left of the food.

A familiar longing for her surfaced, but he ignored it. *She's a virgin, for Chrissakes. I can't give her what she needs. She needs a devoted boyfriend, not a part-time lover.*

"Ready for your big surprise?"

Her eyes held such hope he answered yes, though he steeled himself for God knew what she might spring on him. She held out a box wrapped in gold and burgundy paper, with a gold bow on top. He opened it and was pleased to find what was inside.

"A camera. Looks like an older model," he added, noting the odd design. There was also a black leather case, a little beat-up looking, with the previous owner's initials engraved

on it in gold lettering. The camera itself was in good condi-
tion, and he turned it over in his hands, inspecting it.

"It's vintage, from the 'forties, as far I know. I got it at a
pawn shop downtown. I thought you might find it interesting."

"I do. I can't wait to try it. And you got film, too. Thank
you."

He placed the camera in its case and the film canisters
back in the box, then leaned over to hug her. She whispered
in his ear, her lips brushing the sensitive skin there. "You're
welcome, Zac."

It was a simple thing to say, yet her voice held the promise
of so much more.

At Amanda's insistence, they went down to the water to
take some shots with his birthday gift. The winding path to
the lake was strewn with boulders, and they passed running
children and slow-moving dog walkers as they made their
way to the beach area. More a stretch of sandy pebbles than a
true beach, they picked a dry spot where she set out a large
towel. He sat on it and began loading the film into the camera,
checking the settings and making adjustments. When he
looked up a few minutes later, his breath caught at the sight
of Amanda standing at the water's edge. She had shed her
clothes except for a turquoise bikini, which tied with a string
at each hip and one between her breasts.

For a full minute he sat watching her, the noises and activity on the lake fading away. The sight of her was intoxicating
as she bent to pick up a small rock, causing his thoughts to go
in a direction he knew he should avoid. She skipped the rock
across the water, turning her head to watch as a boat sped by,
causing waves to lap at her feet in quick succession. He rose
to join her, and she turned to him and grinned. "Take some
pictures. I'll be your model."

She began posing, exaggerating her stance and laughing,
until he was laughing too. He watched her through the lens,
adjusting the shutter until he found the right focus. He

snapped away as she bent, twisted, turned and jumped. She waded into the water, and splashed some of it up at him. He moved back, coaching her.

"Yeah, that's it, go a bit deeper. Hey, how about sitting on that rock?"

She climbed up on a boulder, and posed provocatively. She blew kisses at him. A Jet Ski hummed by in the distance, and he waited until the water calmed again so he could get the right shot.

Through the lens, he zoomed in, then zoomed out, experimenting with different angles and focus. The sun glistened off Amanda's hair until a cloud intervened, casting shadows on the water behind her. A splashing in the distance caught his attention, and he looked up to see if it was another boat or other watercraft passing by.

The water was calm, so he looked through the lens again. Something was bobbing in the water, close to the other shore. Horse Tail Reservoir was only a half mile wide in this section, and framed by steep rocks on the other side. He figured it was just a log or something floating, disturbed by the wake of the Jet Ski. He looked again, zooming in on the object. It almost looked like a person, bouncing in the water, flailing. A faint noise reached his ears, a cry. A human voice.

He looked up at the water, but saw nothing. Squinting against the sunlight that had emerged again, he searched the water for a sign of something, or someone. But the surface was calm, waves gently lapping at the pebble-covered shore.

He walked closer to Amanda, who was now watching him with a puzzled expression. "What's wrong?"

Looking through the lens again, he saw a figure, dark head bobbing in the water, arms moving frantically. "It looks like somebody out on the water. Look," he handed her the camera, and she held it to her eye.

"I don't see anyone. Where is it?"

He pointed in the direction of a large pile of boulders near an oak tree on the far shore. "Right by the opposite shore, below that gnarled tree."

She handed the camera back, shaking her head. Another look, and he zoomed in closer this time. There was a distant shout, and the word, "Help!" reached his ears.

"Can you hear that? Someone's in trouble."

He cocked his head, but the cry had faded. He shaded his eyes with a hand, but saw only water. The Jet Ski came back, headed in the opposite direction, passing right by the spot where he had seen the figure. He watched through the camera lens as the Jet Ski drove past, the wake causing the figure in the water to bob more vigorously.

"Why didn't he stop? What an ass."

Amanda was looking at him with an odd expression. He handed her the camera again. "Look though that and tell me you don't see a person out there, in the water."

She stared for a moment holding the camera to her eyes, then handed it back with a shrug. "Sorry. I don't see anyone out there."

The crazy thing was, he didn't either, until he looked through the camera. It looked like a woman, or a child, out there, drowning.

Am I losing it? What the hell?

He began snapping pictures, zooming in closer and closer, more certain with each shot that he was seeing a person in trouble. But every time he looked up from the camera, he saw nothing but water. He looked up and down the beach to see if anyone nearby had a boat or Jet Ski, so he could get out there to help, or at least see what it was. Everyone he saw had come on foot, and there were no lifeguards on this part of the lake.

There was only one thing left to do. Thanking the universe that he was wearing boxers, he stripped down and threw his Tee shirt and jeans on the towel. He glanced at Amanda, whose eyes showed surprise and something else that looked like desire.

"What are you doing?"

He handed her the camera. "Take a picture when I get close to the other side. I have to see for myself what's out there."

She nodded, and he waded into the water. It had been years since he'd even been in a pool, but he was a good swimmer in high school, even worked as a life guard one summer at a community pool. He dove in to the murky water, which felt refreshing for a moment but soon turned cold. Chill bumps rose on his skin each time his arms came out of the water. He paced himself, keeping an eye out for watercraft.

He moved quickly but at a steady pace. He didn't want to get winded in case he had to carry the victim to shore. The sun played hide-and-seek with the clouds, changing the surface of the water from deep teal to almost black and back again. His breath was becoming more ragged, but he pushed on.

When he could clearly see the leaves of the tree on the cliff, he slowed to look around. Treading water, he looked back at the beach, and saw Amanda standing on the rock, the camera at her face. He looked around in the water, and saw nothing. A fish jumped to the surface, startling him, and he noticed tiny insects coming to rest on the water as it stilled.

"I must be seeing things. Maybe it's a flashback from my wilder days…"

Still treading water, he moved closer to the cliff just to be sure he hadn't missed anything. After several minutes he gave up and started back toward the beach. A boat cruised by the beach at a slow speed, the passengers waving to the people onshore. He looked back at the cliff and the tree every few feet, but still saw nothing in the water.

When he reached the shore, Amanda handed him the towel. "So did you see anything out there?"

"Nope. Did you see anything but me in the camera?"

"No. Just that boat of partiers that cruised by a minute ago."

He rubbed the towel through his bushy hair, which would probably be hell to comb through later. Aware that his nipples were standing up from the chill and being perused by his companion, he threw on his shirt. Pulling the jeans up over his wet boxers, he looked back at the water one last time.

"Okay. I don't know what's going on here, but I think we'd better tell the ranger or the lake patrol, just to be safe. Maybe someone else has seen something."

"Sure. Let's go."

She picked up her clothes and dressed, then began gathering their things. He tested the camera again, looking out at where he'd just been. There it was again, head bobbing just above the water. He looked at the lake with his own eyes, to find a calm surface. Another boat sped by, unconcerned by any objects nearby. He placed the camera back in its case and hurried up the path, Amanda following.

He was reminded once again that he hated surprises. Especially when they made no sense.

~*~

Amanda followed Zac into the ranger's office, though she had no idea if she would be any help. He was convinced he'd seen someone out on the lake in trouble, but she'd seen nothing but boats and Jet Skis. She hated seeing him upset, though, so she stood close by while he explained what happened to the Park ranger.

The ranger immediately grabbed his hand-held radio to alert the patrol boat already on the water. "Thanks for reporting that, sir. We'll check it out right away."

There wasn't much else to do after that, so Zac drove them back to where her car was parked near the picnic area. Her excitement at giving him his birthday gift had faded, along with it the hope that he might ask her to spend the evening with him, celebrating his twenty-third birthday.

"So you have big plans for tonight, Zac?" she asked, crossing her fingers where he couldn't see them.

"Uhh...I have to work the bar until nine. Mike and some other guys were gonna take me out after."

"Oh."

"But I really enjoyed lunch. Thanks again for the camera, I love it. It's really cool."

Well, that's worth something. He loves it.

"My pleasure. What are friends for?"

She wanted to be much more than friends with Zac Daley, but he had kept her at a polite distance for months now. When they first met at a frat party last fall, they sped past a polite distance in hurry. Their mutual attraction was instant and scorching—she had never been so attracted to anyone, though Zac was so not her usual type. His wild brown hair and beard, tie-dyed tee shirts and sandals, marked him as what her uptight parents would call a "hippie". But they would never look past his appearance to see what a kind, funny, brave person he was.

But she knew. She also knew they were meant to be together, even if he wasn't ready to admit it yet. He proclaimed to be a confirmed bachelor, preferring to stay single, unattached. But there was something in his eyes when she turned to catch him looking at her. A look that made her tingle, and then ache from some deep, hidden place in her soul.

She would get through to him somehow, some way. Until then, she would be the best friend a guy could have. Which didn't mean she was above flirting now and then, just to keep things interesting.

He parked the car and she got out, enjoying the feel of the sun on her skin. She still wore her bikini top and cut off denim shorts, and though her skin was fair, she had begun to tan. From the corner of her eye, she saw him checking out her legs as she walked, and she grinned. "Well, have fun tonight with the guys. Happy birthday."

She leaned in for a hug, and held on. His beard tickled her forehead, and she turned to plant a kiss on his cheek before he could pull away. His dark eyes looked into hers and for a split second, she thought he might kiss her back. But he pulled away, and squeezed her hand.

"Thanks, Amanda. Now get goin' before I'm late for work."

She got into her dusty orange Ford Pinto and turned the engine, leaning over to open the windows. Zac watched her, lounging against his VW Beetle. She waved and blew him a kiss, and drove away.

And not for the first time, she wondered how much longer she had to get him to admit he wanted her as much as she wanted him. He had mentioned going back home soon to New Jersey, but wouldn't he have done that by now if he was serious? As she turned onto the highway back to Fort Winston, she sent up a silent prayer that she would find a way to touch Zac's heart before he disappeared from her life altogether.

2 Images

Peggy Bresky placed the last of two hundred envelopes in the box, all stamped and ready to mail. Her sons looked up at her with hopeful eyes, pleading silently for release from their sentence. It was a gorgeous summer day, and she knew both boys were anxious to be outside playing. Instead, she'd kept them in to help fill and stamp envelopes for the invitations to her upcoming speaking engagement, and they had done so with minimal grumbling.

"All right, go on outside. But be back in an hour. Then we'll go to town and get these mailed."

Sam, the youngest, knocked over his chair in his haste to leave. His older brother Howie picked it up, then followed, shaking his finger and putting it to his mouth. He was nursing his first paper cut, and Peggy smiled, knowing it wouldn't be his last.

She sighed, content in the knowledge she had taken a huge step toward her goal. If she had her way, by the end of summer all of Fort Winston would know her name. She had always imagined what it would feel like, to be the one who would make a difference. There would be many letters to open, full of invitations for her to speak, followed by donations for her cause. She was going to clean up this town, and there wasn't a moment to waste. The influx of illegal drugs had become an epidemic lately, especially since they started having rock and roll concerts at the local college, and she wasn't about to stand by while her beloved Fort Winston turned into some sort of hippie commune.

She had taken on the cause when the ugly specter of drug abuse had affected her nephew. She knew then she could not stand by idly and let other families suffer as she and her brother Walter had. Though Jeffrey was back to normal now, thank the Lord, it might not be so easy for some people.

Temptation was everywhere nowadays, especially at Fort Winston University, where her daughter attended.

"Rotten kids, with their Devil's music," she muttered, heading to the pantry. Reaching behind a sack of flour on the floor, she retrieved the bottle of vodka she'd stashed, her own private indulgence. At the counter, she poured some of the vodka over ice, followed by a splash of lemon lime soda. She took a long sip, leaning against the counter while the warmth slid down to her stomach.

Replacing the vodka to its hiding place, she finished her drink and washed the glass. Her husband wouldn't approve of her imbibing in the afternoon like this. Victor had his one beer every evening after supper, and that was it. But what he didn't know about her habits while he was at work, wouldn't hurt him.

Switching on the television, she turned the channel to the midday news. Since taking on her cause against illegal drug use, she devoured every news program and newspaper article she could find, hoping to learn more about it. Who was using it, and where was it coming from? And how could it be stopped?

She looked out the window at her sons playing in the yard. They were having a competition to see who could swing the highest from a rope tied to the large oak tree. At ten and thirteen, they were still too young to know what dangers lurked on every corner, and it was her duty to protect them. It was a full time job, no doubt. To her credit, though, she had managed to raise her daughter Amanda to college age without much trouble. So far.

As if summoned, her daughter's Ford Pinto pulled into to the driveway. She waved to her brothers as she emerged from the car, carrying a cooler.

"So that's what happened to the pierogis," Peggy whispered, getting up to open the door. Amanda smiled as she passed her mother, heading for the kitchen.

"Thanks, Mom. There's still some food in here, if you're hungry."

"And who else have you been feeding? Not that I mind…"

Her daughter didn't answer, but kept busy unloading the cooler. Peggy stood waiting, wondering why it was a tough question.

"Ohh…just a friend of mine. It was his birthday today."

"I see."

As a mother, she had learned that sometimes what you didn't say was as powerful as any spoken words. She waited, watching the girl who looked so much like her, what she looked like years ago, before time and hardship took their toll. Except for her height; she took after her father in that regard.

Amanda looked at her and shrugged. "It was my friend Zac, and I hadn't seen him in a while. There, are you satisfied? Jeesh."

"Don't get smart with me, young lady. And next time ask before you take whatever you want. Now I have to re-plan dinner."

"Okay, sorry. I'll help. Guess I'm staying home tonight, anyway."

"Oh, were you planning on seeing this boy tonight, too? Which one is he?"

Her question was met with a groan, and Amanda headed toward the stairs and her bedroom. "Mom, I'm twenty years old. Give me a break."

As her daughter stomped her way up the stairs, Peggy called after her. "You haven't answered my questions, Mandy."

Before the door slammed shut, she heard, "You haven't met him. And I'm keeping it that way."

Her intuition told her there was something going on, but so far, Amanda had been a good girl and she had to count on that continuing. Her daughter attended church regularly, came home at a decent hour most nights, and seemed to hang with a pretty good group of kids. But she was nearly twenty-one, and Peggy could feel a slipping of the tenuous control she held over her daughter. Perhaps she'd held on too long. Some of her neighbor's kids had left home or had been sleeping around long before Amanda's age. To her mind, just because others did that didn't make it right, and it was her duty to see that all her children had the best possible start in life. If that meant keeping a tight rein on their activities, so be it.

She stood in the living room, looking out the window but thinking of the change in Mandy's behavior. It was little things—her moodiness, the faraway look she had in her eyes, subtle changes in the way she dressed. Most of all it was her tendency to keep secrets, which she had never done before. They had always been close, but now Amanda was moving away from her, and it seemed to have begun when she first mentioned this Zac character.

Were they more than friends? As far as she knew, her daughter was still a virgin, and planned to stay that way until she married.

"As it should be," she muttered, walking back to the pantry. Anxiety suddenly took hold, and she grabbed her glass again from the counter.

It was a two-shot afternoon if she'd ever seen one. Cleaning up Fort Winston could wait for another hour or two.

~*~

Zac was up early, anxious to get to the ranger's station to find out if anyone had reported something, or someone, in the lake. He'd cut short his birthday celebration and went home to bed, but sleep had eluded him. Images of a young girl in the water, splashing in panic, kept repeating in his mind. It had been too far to see much detail, so he had no idea whether what he saw really was a girl. But that's what his instincts told him.

Or maybe he was just delusional. The stress of facing his impending big life decisions were taking a toll. *Maybe I just need to start over somewhere, anywhere. I've got no strings, nothing holding me back.*

But something else had kept him awake, staring into the darkness of his room. Amanda, looking hotter than ever in her bikini, or leaning over to hand him a slice of cake. It was his decision to be nothing more than friends, but he'd never imagined how difficult that would be to carry out.

Or how much he'd come to regret it.

Shortly after eight, he turned onto Buckhorn Road, wishing he'd grabbed a second cup of coffee. It was Saturday, and they were bound to be bombarded later with summer crowds on the lake, so he thought it best to get there early. It was none of his business what they'd found, if anything, but for his own peace of mind he had to know.

The parking lot held several cars already, early bird fishermen racing to get the best spots on the narrow reservoir. He walked up to the small building that housed the Park ranger's office, a bait and tackle store, and a boat rental. The marina below was busy, every slip filled with watercraft of various shapes and sizes.

It took a few minutes to get the ranger's attention, focused as the man was on his hand-held radio. Whoever it was he was speaking with was excited, having busted a group of kids who'd camped on one of the beaches illegally, and the local police were being called in to check for drugs and underage drinking. The kids were dispersing quickly as the Lake Patrol was attempting to write citations, and the ranger was juggling the radio with the phone in an effort to coordinate all of it.

Then he looked up from his desk at Zac, who probably looked to him to be the ringleader of the renegade group of partying kids.

Guess I should've combed my hair this morning, but what the hell...

"Hey, uh, sir," Zac started, clearing his throat. "I was wondering if they ever found anything, or I mean, anyone in trouble on the lake yesterday? I came in here and reported seeing a person in the water who needed help."

"Not that I know of. There's been no report of injuries or rescue. Just parties on the beach and a few boats that had to be towed."

"Okay, thanks."

Relief spread through him. *Okay, so it was a fluke. The film will come up with nothing. It was just stress, or maybe I need my eyes checked.*

If there had been anyone out there, the film would show it. He'd dropped it off at the drive-through film kiosk to be developed, even though the roll had not been finished. He no longer had access to the campus darkroom, or he'd have checked it out himself, right away. He needed to see those photos as soon as possible, for vindication.

He made his way down the hill, turning into the lower lot where the picnic pavilion was. He had to check it out, just to be sure he wasn't going crazy. The vintage camera sat on the passenger seat, loaded and ready. As soon as his feet hit the trail to the beach, he was squinting against the morning sun to see the far shore. His eyes searched for the gnarled oak tree, directly above the spot where he had seen her.

Drowning Girl. That's what he'd named her, but he hoped he'd never see her again.

The beach was deserted, so he walked to the water's edge, camera in hand. He adjusted the lens as he held it to his eye, and took in a breath. Though the surface was a calm green sheet of glass, the dark head bobbed just above the water, as if being tossed about in a wave pool. He could see her arms thrashing, more frantically as her head submerged below the water.

This can't be real. What are the chances?

He looked up, over the camera and out at the distant shore. Nothing. No sign of a person, animal, or watercraft of any kind.

Looking through the lens again, he zoomed in as far as possible. The figure in the water turned, looking straight at him, and mouthed the word, "Help".

Though the sun beat down, he felt a chill. His stomach clenched, forcing him to take a deep breath to calm himself. He watched the figure through the lens, certain now it was a girl, probably in her late teens. She was actually waving, as though she knew he could see her. He stared, heart pounding, brain trying to comprehend how this could happen. *How someone could be drowning in the lake for two days, unseen by anyone but me?*

Glancing up, he saw murky green water, undisturbed. Untouched. But through his lens he saw a person in trouble, who could not be saved. He'd never felt so helpless, not since that horrible day when he first came to Colorado. He couldn't save Gina in time, either, and that was something he would never forget. The fact that it had been an accident did nothing to ease his guilt, or erase his pain completely. He was the one who'd fallen asleep at the wheel, and caused the crash, yet he was the only one who survived.

He stood on the beach, frozen, unable to move and jittery at the same time. Closing his eyes, he took a deep, calming breath, listening to the gentle waves at his feet. Carried on the breeze was a faint cry, the same he heard the day before. A girl crying for help.

The sound faded as a boat approached. He looked through the lens again, snapping a photo as the lake patrol boat cruised right by the girl in the water, as if she wasn't there. Unconcerned, searching for unlicensed fishermen or unruly teens, the driver of the boat continued on.

Hair prickled on the back of his neck, and he sensed he was being watched. The sound of a voice behind him made him jump, and he turned toward it. But he was still alone on the beach, leaving him to wonder if he truly was losing his mind.

"Enough. This is crazy."

Placing the lens cap back on the camera, he trudged up the trail. It was a great temptation to toss the thing in a trash bin, but Amanda would be crushed if he did, so when he got to his car, he threw it on the back seat. He didn't want to even look at the cursed thing, so he jammed the VW into gear and took off, driving fast. He had to get away from Horse Tail Reservoir as soon as possible.

He was a few miles down the road before he realized he had a death grip on the steering wheel. It had been four years since the accident, and he thought he'd made peace with it, had overcome the anguish that once drove him to excess. He'd been sober for three years now, never touching drugs of any kind, drinking only a beer or two on occasion. But today a switch had been flipped somehow, and a dark craving for an escape of some kind gnawed at him.

He looked in the rearview mirror as the rugged red peaks of the Horse Tail Range that towered above the lake came into view. He'd just avoid the place, never come back. He would forget all about it, in time.

Unless she shows up in the photos I took. Then what?

~*~

Amanda checked her watch for the fourteenth time that hour. Convinced it must be broken, she tapped it and put it to her ear, but the thing was still humming. The morning had seemed to last a lifetime, and she wanted to leave already. Needed to leave. She knew Zac often spent Sunday afternoons at the park, taking photos for his portfolio, and there was no way she was going to miss seeing him.

The church service was long over, but her mother had been mobbed by a crowd, all asking questions about the upcoming rally against illegal drug use. It was Peggy's latest cause-du-jour, and she had really taken this one to heart. More than once, Amanda had been physically examined and questioned at length, though she had never touched drugs, nor alcohol, for that matter. During allergy season, she had a hard time convincing her overly suspicious mother that her reddened eyes were a result of hay fever, not smoking grass.

As if I would. What's the big deal?

She regretted her decision that morning to ride along with her family instead of driving herself to church. She spotted her father in conversation with the pastor; her brothers ran past, chasing another boy, laughing. While she stood against the wall, alone, waiting patiently. But that was her, the good girl. Forever doing what she was told, what was expected of her.

So why did her heart feel rebellious lately? She looked down at her prim, conservative church clothes—a pink cotton summer shift with a high neckline, skirt just to the knee. But underneath...no one else knew she was wearing the laciest, silkiest black panties and bra, with a garter belt to match. It was her own private indulgence, a way to express the passion she felt without being judged by the world.

Taking her time, she walked to the family station wagon which was parked under a tree. Images of Zac filled her mind, a fantasy so well developed, she knew it by heart. Like a favorite movie or television show, she recalled it whenever she was alone. Imagining his face when he saw her lacy lingerie, how he would touch her, and kiss her. What it would feel like to take his body into hers for the first time.

They had made out a few times back when they first met, so she knew the taste of him. His arms, strong and muscular, had held her tight, so close she felt his heart beat. The last time, in his dorm room, she'd even felt the hardness in his jeans pressing against her and it made her dizzy with desire. When he'd put his long, slender fingers under her shirt, she thought she'd pass out from excitement.

Until you ruined it, you idiot.

What had she been thinking? Blurting out, "I'm a virgin"? *Way to ruin the best thing you ever had.*

Maybe it was nerves. Maybe she thought he would be honored, and happy to be her first lover. But that wasn't how it played out, and she still didn't understand why.

Opening the car door, she sat on the edge of the driver's seat, watching the crowd of church goers slowly disperse. A dull ache began in her stomach, weighing on her. The look of surprise on Zac's face when she had revealed her sexual in-experience still haunted her. He'd pulled away, smoothing her hair and clothing as though she were a porcelain doll about to break. Despite her urging to continue, he shook his head and stood up, having decided her fate.

"I can't. I'm not the guy you should be with, your first time. You're…a special girl, Amanda."

"But I'm ready. I *want* you to be my first. Don't you want me?"

His coffee-dark eyes had looked into hers for a long moment, before he took her hand in his. She fought back tears, not wanting to seem immature. Her cheeks were hot with embarrassment. She'd never imagined he'd say no to going all the way.

His voice barely above a whisper, he'd tried to comfort her. "Of course I do, or we wouldn't be here like this. But…you have to understand, I don't do relationships. I'm not the boyfriend type, and you deserve better than just casual sex. I probably shouldn't have let it get this far. I mean, if I had known-"

The pain of his rejection boiled over into anger. She withdrew her hand from his as if it burned. "So you wouldn't have even *kissed* me if you knew I was a virgin? Well, I wouldn't have kissed you if I had known you were a jerk."

She had walked out of his dorm room, head held high. He protested, tried to explain his position, but she kept going. It was only as she reached her car that she turned to face him. He took her into his arms and kissed her hard, her anger subsiding as she melted into his embrace. He broke the kiss and looked down at her, emotion and passion evident in his eyes.

"I will never regret kissing you, Amanda. But I won't be responsible for breaking your heart."

But you already have.

She wanted to yell at him, punch him, to hurt him back. But she couldn't. She knew he was afraid of hurting her, that he thought he was doing the right thing. But that didn't take away her pain, so "I understand," was all she could manage.

"So…still friends, right?"

Her lips were moist from his kiss, and she fought the urge to press up against him, and demand another. Was this the last kiss they would ever have? She couldn't stand the thought, didn't want to give in, and she wasn't about to give up.

"Of course, Zac. I have to go now."

He stood in the parking lot, watching her leave. As she drove away, wiping the tears that fell freely, she knew they were not in vain. A man who doesn't want you wouldn't be standing there, watching you leave with longing written all over his face. He just had some kind of issues to work through, and when he was ready, she would be there.

His rejection had been crushing, though she knew he had her best interests at heart. Her wild-haired, hippie-ish party guy turned out to be a gentleman, but that's not what she wanted. She wanted him to throw her on the bed and take her, with passionate abandon. The fact that he was so different than the preppie, straight-laced boys she usually dated was what had drawn her to him in the first place, and he had shown more care and concern for her than any of them ever had. Perhaps too much concern, because here she was, months later, still waiting.

Her desire and affection for him had grown over that time, but her patience was diminishing. And to top it off, now that he had graduated, she had no idea if he was going to stay in Fort Winston, or disappear, taking her heart along with him.

Her parents appeared with both her brothers in tow behind them. She started the car with her key, anxious to be somewhere else.

Anxious to be *someone* else.

3 Possibilities

Zac stared at the photos laid out on the table, still not believing his eyes. Of the twenty shots he had taken that day on the lake, only six were of the spot where he had seen the Drowning Girl. Four of those definitely showed there had been something in the water that day.

What it was remained to be determined.

He held one of the photos close, squinting down his nose. A blurry, brown shape of something was on the surface of the water. It could be a branch, or an animal. But when he looked at it, though his rational mind tried to explain it as something sensible, his eyes still saw what he believed it to be—a human.

What really tripped him out was the last photo in the bunch, where the patrol boat sped right by the head in the water, as though it were invisible.

This makes no sense. Amanda couldn't see it, so why did I?

He looked up from his table, wondering where she was. She'd agreed to meet him at six, but she was late. That wasn't like her, and he hoped she remembered the right place, their favorite pizza joint downtown. They'd eaten there many times, including on their first date, almost a year ago.

Wow. In a few months, it'll be a year since we met at that frat party. Thinking of that night always made him grin, how she laughed at his jokes, how natural it felt to hold her. Their chemistry was explosive, and she was the best kisser he'd ever met. What a bummer it was to find out a few weeks later she was a virgin, and not the experienced young woman she had seemed.

But the scariest thing, what really made him back off, was the look in her eyes. She adored him, and he didn't want her falling in love. He just could not give of himself, not the way she wanted. He kept his relationships, if you could call them that, open for a reason. He never wanted to feel again the way he felt after Gina died. So falling in love was out of the question.

He should have left it at goodbye. But when Amanda walked out of his dorm that night, the last time they made out, he knew he still wanted her in his life. They were friends, and she understood him like no one else. He didn't know why; they had so little in common. It was just a feeling, and he wasn't willing to let it go completely.

It might have been selfish of him, but she had acquiesced and they settled into a warm friendship. It was tough holding back on the physical aspects, especially when she seemed to taunt him, but there was no other way. Becoming sexually involved would surely cause complications, and bad feelings for both of them.

"Hey, Fuzzy. Sorry I'm late."

It was her pet nickname for him, and though it had annoyed him at first, now it made him smile. She sat in the chair opposite him, and poured a glass of root beer from the pitcher on the table. Her manner was cheery, as usual, helping to lighten the serious funk he had been in for days.

"No problemo. I just needed you to look at something, and tell me what you think."

He handed her the photos, all twenty of them. He wanted to see her reaction when she reached the ones he was questioning. He sat back, munching on a slice of pizza, watching her face. She examined them slowly, smiling at the ones of her in the bikini.

She knows she looks hot, damn her.

"Okay, what's this thing here? I didn't see that in the camera."

She pointed at the brown shape in the water, where the Drowning Girl had been.

"Good, you see it too. I was beginning to think I'd lost my mind. Or my eyesight was going bad."

She turned the photo sideways, then held it close, nose scrunched as she peered at the object. "It might be a log, right? But it really looks like…"

"Like a person in the water. A drowning girl."

Her copper-dark eyes stared at him, long lashes stark against her fair skin. She shook her head, ginger hair falling from behind her ears.

"No, it can't be. We couldn't see anything, and you said the lake patrol didn't either. The only time you saw it was—"

"Through the camera you gave me. It doesn't make sense. But you know what's worse?"

Her lips were open, covered in sugar-pink lip gloss. They trembled slightly, as though she was afraid to say what she imagined could be worse. One word came out, a whisper. "What?"

"I saw it—her—again Saturday morning. After the ranger told me they'd found nothing, I went back to the beach with the camera, and it happened all over again."

"No way."

"Yes, way. I'm serious."

She looked at the photos again, having separated the ones with the mysterious object. He knew they could only tell so much from the photos. They both spoke at once, saying almost the same thing.

"We have to investigate—"

"This doesn't prove anything—"

They spent the next hour discussing the possibilities, from the outrageous to the plausible. He felt some relief at being able to discuss what he saw with someone, without fear of repercussion.

"Amanda, I'm so glad you believe me, but don't tell anyone about this until we find out more about it."

"Of course. They'd think we were crazy, right? Don't worry. But how will we ever find out what it was?"

"I don't know, but I'm not leaving Fort Winston until I find out."

Her smile faded, lips forming a tight line. "Were you planning on leaving soon, before this happened?"

Why did he suddenly feel like a trapped rat?

"I guess I'll have to move on sometime. For now, I'm just trying to figure out my options. I'm working on my portfolio, in case the photography thing works out, too. Hey, maybe I can become a ghost hunter."

His joke was meant to ease the tension, but the thought of a possible ghost had not occurred to him until that moment. Amanda's smile returned, and she joined in.

"Yeah, that's it. Zac Daley, Expert Ghost Photographer."

"Hey, ya gotta have an angle, right?"

~*~

"I'd like to thank you all for coming today. It warms my heart to know I'm not alone in this fight to protect the young people of Powder County."

Peggy Bresky stood taller than her five feet, two inches that night. The meeting room was filled, every seat. Concerned parents, grandparents, and even a few teens all looked to her for guidance and information. The turnout surprised even her, but she considered it a sign that she was on the right path. Speaking from the podium, she launched into her well-rehearsed speech.

"This is an informational meeting, to let the community know what can be done to address the recent influx of illegal drugs, and the resulting problems some residents of Fort Winston have faced. Some of you may have already experienced the heartbreak and disruption that is addiction, and the chaos even recreational use of these so-called "street drugs" can cause. Unfortunately, it is becoming all too common these days. Our hearts go out to those who have had problems, but let me assure you, help is on the way. Those of you who don't know anything about illegal drugs, we welcome you, as well. When part of a community suffers, it affects everyone, in one way or another."

The faces in the audience were hopeful, giving her the strength to overcome her nerves. She believed in her heart she was doing the right thing, and the validation felt good. She glanced over at her husband, Victor, who was in the corner speaking in whispers to her brother, Walt. Both had told her they expected a good turnout, but she'd been too nervous to believe it. She took a deep breath and continued, the tension finally uncoiling in her stomach.

"To give you all a bit of background on the severity of this problem in Powder County, we are pleased to have with us tonight our Sheriff, Walter Jackson."

Polite applause followed the introduction, and her brother took his place in front of the podium. He was a big man, and he had the same red hair as she, though his was shot through with whitish-gray streaks. Being related to the county Sheriff had always been a source of pride for her, especially after he gained notoriety for busting that Russian spy ring last fall. But now she realized just how much leverage his position might have for her cause. Walter was well-regarded in the town, and though few knew it, he had personally experienced a family crisis due to drugs, when his youngest son entered rehabilitation the year before.

His personal conviction came through as he spoke, explaining the various drugs his staff had recently confiscated. "Marijuana is the least of it, folks, believe me. Not to say it isn't harmful. But nowadays, they even spike that stuff with other chemicals, such as PCP, or Angel Dust...these kids might think they're in for a relaxing, mellow high, and end up flipping out and hurting others, or themselves. And then, there's the issue of pharmaceuticals, pills they've stolen from Grandma's medicine cabinet..."

The crowd shifted in their seats, some looking shocked as Walt went on, including statistics from the local hospital about drug-related illnesses and injuries. The faces of the audience had gone from hopeful to horrified, and Peggy couldn't be happier. Horrified people were more likely to commit their time, money and resources to a cause they cared about.

She realized Walt was winding up his presentation, and she joined him at the podium.

"And I can't think of a better person to lead the charge against drugs in our town, than this little lady. Let's hear it for Peggy Bresky."

The applause made her heart swell. She bowed to the audience, and swatted Walt on the arm, then hugged him. When the clapping died down, she spoke.

"Thank you so much. I promise I will do my best. Now, the next order of business will be organizing our volunteers. We have sign-up sheets at the back of the room, listing what positions we need and how much time is required for each. Please leave your name and phone number on the sheet, so that we may contact you and get started. Remember, if we all pull together, anything is possible."

The crowd began to rise from their seats. She was pleased with how it went, but knew it was just the beginning of something great. "And don't forget the rally in the park, on the Fourth of July, at noon. I hope you will all come out and support our cause, even if you can't volunteer."

The next half hour was coffee, donuts, and chatting with the stragglers. She found herself once again the center of attention, just as she had at church on Sunday. She felt like celebrating, and wished she'd brought along her flask in her purse. A nip in her coffee sure would cap off the night. She'd just have to wait until Vic and the kids were asleep, then she'd have her own private toast to a successful kick-off meeting.

~*~

"Score. Empty house."

Amanda threw her purse on the sofa and headed for the kitchen. Being in the house alone was a rare occasion, and she had no idea how long it would be until her family returned and the place was full of noise and clutter. Her mother had said something about a meeting, so maybe she had a few hours.

She grabbed a diet soda from the fridge and a cookie from the jar on the counter. Her mind was spinning from her discussions with Zac, considering all angles of the situation. The mystery of what was in the photos was his main concern; hers was the fact that he said he wouldn't leave until he solved it.

Which put her in an awkward position. He'd asked for her help, but once the mystery was solved he'd be gone. She wanted to help him, and was curious to find out what the heck he had actually seen. But she hated the idea of losing him, having him move back to New Jersey, or somewhere else far away.

With a sigh, she retrieved her purse and climbed the stairs, munching on the cookie. When she reached her room, she closed the door and latched it, out of habit. Her mother thought nothing of barging in after a courtesy knock, whether she was welcome or not.

She slipped into her summer cotton pajamas, a ruffled tank and shorts set. She put a Fleetwood Mac album on her record player and lay back on the bed, recalling how excited Zac had seemed. He was clearly disturbed by what had happened with the camera, but it also put a fire under him, which was a welcome change. After graduation, he'd been quiet, not his usual jokey self. She'd suggested activities to get him out of his room and motivated again, like hiking up Powder Keg Canyon, or riding bikes through the park. He usually declined, saying he was busy. Doing what, was the question.

She knew he occasionally dated other girls, and she'd had a few dates with other guys. But true to his word, Zac didn't have steady relationships with any of them. Which still did not lessen the sting she felt at the thought of him with someone else, and she wondered if he ever felt the same about her.

This crazy obsession of his lately had proved one thing—she was the one he called on, when he needed help. No one else.

He needs me. That has possibilities…

Comforted, she propped up her pillows and picked up the book on her nightstand. She would figure it all out tomorrow, when they went back to the lake to look around. Tonight, she just wanted peace.

4 Appearances

"This is becoming a habit," Zac said as they rounded the curve up to the parking lot at Horse Tail Reservoir. "It's starting to feel like I live here. Maybe I should just pitch a tent and make myself at home."

Amanda smirked, and rolled her eyes. He still thought she was damn cute, even when she made fun of him. "Until the ranger kicks you out, then you can come camp on my lawn."

"Oh yeah, your Dad would love that, I'm sure."

"Actually it's Mom we'd have to worry about. She can be fierce."

"Of course, she's a redhead, isn't she?"

His question was met with another smirk, and she stuck her tongue out at him for emphasis. He'd only seen her parents from afar, when they had attended Fort Winston University's graduation ceremony. A friend's daughter had graduated the same day as Zac, which was why they were there. But they'd left before Amanda had a chance to introduce him.

He often wondered if she had purposefully avoided introducing him to her parents, but he never asked. Probably a bad idea, anyway. Parents and anyone over the age of thirty tended to look at him and conclude he was a drug-addled hippie. He wasn't going to cut his hair and stop wearing ripped jeans for anyone, so why cause drama?

It was late afternoon, and the sky had clouded up. Fluffy piles of white with dark blue bottoms were stacking overhead, threatening rain. Zac and Amanda stood on the cliff next to the picnic pavilion, staring down at the water, empty of boats and swimmers. The only sound was the wind rippling over the water and causing the nearby trees to sway, moving their branches in protest as if warning them to leave.

Zac felt a shiver down his back. "Looks like rain coming. The boats have cleared off." He'd been anxious to get there, to explore again, but now his legs seemed frozen. "I want to go down there, but…"

She looked up at him with the same anxiety on her face as he felt in his gut. "I know. It's like you want to know, but you don't."

"I wish there was something else we could do. If I keep seeing the same thing, it won't answer our questions."

Removing the camera from its case, he uncapped the lens cover and looked through. Focusing on the opposite shore, he searched up and down in the area he had seen the girl. Today he saw nothing.

"You know, Zac, maybe there is something else we can do. I've never been, but I heard there's an old Forestry road over there, that leads to that cliff." She was pointing to the rocks above the spot where the girl in the water had been. "Kids used to jump into the lake from there until they closed it off, but I bet we can get close enough to go in on foot."

"Maybe. Think we have time to get over there before the rain starts?"

She glanced at the clouds scudding overhead. "Maybe. Sometimes they keep going, sometimes they drown you."

He frowned at her choice of words, and she put a hand to her mouth.

"Oops. You know what I mean. Let's go."

It took another hour for them to travel up the Forestry road on the other side of the lake. Gravel turned to dirt, and the road narrowed down to become little more than a wide trail. He parked when they came to a dead end, where a chain suspended between two posts was blocking the road. Hanging on the chain, and flapping in the breeze, was a sign that said, "No Trespassing".

"I seem to have knack for finding every one of these in the county," he quipped, pointing to the sign. "But with this ghost, or whatever it is—I now know how my friend Sarah felt, when she saw something weird she couldn't explain."

"Yeah, and it didn't work out so well for her."

"Well, in the end, it did. But yeah, that's a time I'd rather forget."

Amanda had been by his side throughout his adventures last year when he'd helped her Uncle Walter, the Sheriff of Powder County, capture a spy who had set up camp in Fort Winston. His friend Sarah McKenn and her boyfriend Chris had been drawn into the situation, and had barely come out of it alive. Zac liked to think he'd helped save them, by telling the Sheriff what he knew about it just in the nick of time. In her eyes, he was always a hero, but his part in the incident had proved it.

They walked on, keeping an eye on the sky. The sun was still above the horizon, and wouldn't set for a few hours. The clouds had thickened to a grey mass, tinged with an orange glow where the evening sun shone through. The trail wound through brush and gnarled trees, and more than a few jackrabbits crossed their path, seeking safety.

The trail flattened out into an open area as they reached the ledge overlooking the lake. He could hear the water lapping against the rocks at the bottom of the cliff, and he looked down, feeling dizzy.

"Whoa," he breathed. "That's steep. You sure kids used to jump off here?"

Amanda peeked over the ledge. "Yep. I know this is the spot, because of that."

She pointed over his shoulder to a pile of huge boulders. On the largest rock was painted "FWU", for Fort Winston University, along with other, less polite graffiti. It was then he noticed the remains of various campfires on the ground, crude circles of stones filled with ashes and burnt wood.

"Okay. This must be the place, then. I'm gonna look around, take some pictures."

She didn't say anything, just wandered off exploring, while he searched in his backpack. This time, he brought two cameras—one was a disposable, cheap thing, the other was the vintage camera that had caused all the trouble.

First, he looked around through the disposable camera, taking shots of the water, the rocks, the campsites. Nothing looked unusual but he couldn't shake the eerie vibe he felt, as though something bad had happened there. He'd never been psychic, and didn't believe in what he couldn't see and prove. But the hair stood up on his neck, and it wasn't caused by the breeze from the oncoming evening storm.

So far, he'd seen nothing strange. He glanced over at Amanda, who was picking flowers, giving him some space. He was switching cameras when he saw something from the corner of his eye, felt someone approaching. Thinking it was her, he asked if she'd seen anything.

There was no answer, so he turned, and saw a young woman, partially hidden by a bush. Her hair was straggly and wet, her tee-shirt torn, her skin mottled with cuts and bruises. His breath left him as he tried to speak, and he looked toward Amanda to call her. When he looked back at the girl, she had vanished.

He found his voice. "Hey, c'mere!"

Amanda ran to him. "What is it? Are you okay?"

He looked around. No, they were still alone. "I saw her. The Drowning Girl."

~*~

Amanda's breath left in a rush. She wanted to believe him, but was afraid to. "There's no one else here. What exactly did you see?"

"She was about your height, standing by that bush. Brown, stringy hair, wet as if she'd been in the water. Her clothes were torn and dirty, and she was all bruised up and looking at me with those eyes…oh, crap, I can't believe this."

Running a hand over his face, he blinked hard. She'd never seen him so freaked out about anything. A hard ball of ice formed in her stomach, as she contemplated the idea of actually seeing a ghost. Her instincts told her that wasn't possible, and she sought to calm him.

"Maybe you've just been thinking about this so much, it's your imagination gone wild. Your brain is trying to fabricate something to answer your questions."

The look he shot her was a mixture of confusion and indignation. "I don't know what to think, but I'm not prone to making shit up, you know that."

She moved closer, touching his arm. "Yes, I do. It's okay. We'll figure it out. Did you get some shots?"

"I did, with the cheap camera. But until that girl appeared, I saw nothing unusual."

He still held the vintage camera in his hand. His dark eyes looked into hers, and for a split second she thought she saw desire there. Now it was her imagination working overtime. They stood close for a moment, her hand still on his arm. She squeezed it, and he relaxed. They were so close, only inches apart. He could kiss her if he wanted to. As the seconds ticked by, she thought he might, because he was looking at her lips like they were a luscious dessert. Then he moved away, licking his own lips.

Feeling awkward, she walked toward the ledge. "If there is some kind of spirit or ghost, maybe she's trying to tell you something."

"Well, I wish she'd just come out with it. Enough with the hide and seek already."

He joined her at the ledge and looked down at the water. Focusing the lens, he began taking shots, turning this way and that. Amanda watched as he moved to the bush where the girl had been, and photographed that, too. A rumble of thunder echoed across the lake, and they both looked skyward.

"We'd better get going, Zac."

"Right. Just one more shot."

A flower fell from the bundle she still held in her hand, landing in the dirt. As she bent to retrieve it, her finger brushed something metal. "What's this?"

Pulling it from the dirt, she held the short metal clip between her fingers toward Zac. It was about three inches long, attached to a leather tag.

"That's a roach clip. Where'd you find it?"

"On the ground, just there." She pointed to the ground, and he took the clip from her, turning it over in his hand.

"There's initials here, on this key tag. 'M.F.'"

"That would be used for smoking pot, right?"

"Yep. It's a nice one. I wonder how they lost it."

He shoved it his backpack, along with the cameras. They were done for the day, and not a moment too soon. Cold drops were splattering on her skin already, hitting the ground with soft, pelting sounds.

They ran to the car, climbing inside just as the skies opened up. It took longer to drive back to the main road than it had to get up there, due to the downpour. By the time they were on the main road back to town, the rain had stopped. An intense peach glow lit the horizon over the Horse Tail Range as the sun set, reminding her that another day had gone by, and she was no closer to Zac than she had been for months.

He pulled up to the pizza shop's parking lot, where they had left her car. He'd been talking about the "Drowning Girl" the whole way back, and she begun to wonder if this obsession of his was healthy. She got out of the car and came around to his side where he leaned out the window.

"Listen, Fuzzy…try to relax about this, okay? I believe you, I really do. But I'm starting to worry. Don't let it freak you out. I almost wish I hadn't given you that damn camera."

He reached for her hand, and held it, rubbing his thumb over her knuckles. Her body reacted with a warm rush, for his simple touch meant so much to her.

"I know, I've been acting like a friggin' lunatic over this. It's probably nothing, right? I guess I better get my shit together."

She didn't know what to say, so she followed her impulse and leaned down to kiss his cheek. Hugging his neck, she laughed. "Yes, but you're my favorite lunatic, you know."

As she drove away, a glance in her rearview mirror told her all she needed to know. He was watching her leave, with a hand to his cheek where she had kissed him.

~*~

Peggy looked around the room, pleased with the group of volunteers she had selected from the list. Seven women, all well-known and active in the community, were attending the first meeting of the newly-formed group she was heading up. No doubt, this lineup would make great progress in a short time. She had hand-picked them from the pool of eager volunteers, and she was more than ready to get the ball rolling. As the ladies settled into their chairs, sharing gossip and tales of childrearing, Peggy called the meeting to order.

"Good afternoon, ladies. Thank you all for coming. I know you're going to be as excited as I am when you hear what we'll be doing over the next several weeks."

First, she asked each one to introduce themselves to the group, and describe any areas of expertise. The women were mostly housewives, except for Wanda, who was a nurse, and Bridget, a school teacher. But even the housewives had skills or connections that would be useful. She made notes as they talked, her mind already spinning with ideas.

They spent the next twenty minutes discussing ways they might get the word out about the upcoming rally in the park. The next few weeks would be crucial to the launching of their campaign, and she wanted to unite them, knowing they would accomplish so much more as a group than as individuals.

"So, ladies, I must tell you I'm impressed. We've quite a talented group here, wouldn't you say?"

There were satisfied smiles and pleasant murmurs all around, so she dove in.

"We can do so much to clean up this town. I think I speak for everyone here when I say that nothing puts fear in to a mother's heart quicker than something that may harm her children, and the presence of these drugs, and those that make them available, is enough to scare me to pieces."

The ladies chatted in agreement, starting to babble about their own fears as parents and concerned citizens. She let them go for a moment, then cleared her throat, regaining their attention. Knowing that appearances are everything, she stood up, holding one of the placards she had made at home.

"So to grab the public's attention, ladies, we need a catch phrase, and a memorable name. Something that will stick in their minds, touch their emotions. So I submit to you our group's moniker, if you all agree, that is."

On the placard were the words, "Mothers Against Illegal Drugs". Below that, the acronym, "M.A.I.D."

There was stunned silence for a moment, and then Wanda, the nurse, clapped her hands and giggled. "I love it. The "M.A.I.D.s" are gonna clean up this town."

Polite laughter followed, and Peggy beamed. It was exactly the slogan she'd come up with, and now they'd think it was their idea. "That's right. What a great slogan that will be."

They made plans to meet twice each week, with events on Saturdays. They would also be active at their various churches, and fliers about the rally would be available to pass out as soon as Peggy could get them printed. One of the ladies was friends with the local printer, and she offered to make some calls. Bridget, who taught at the Junior High, asked to have Walter come speak about the dangers of drugs with the kids who were attending summer school.

Yes, it was all coming together, more quickly than she had hoped. It was unfortunate that Walt's son Jeffrey had fallen into the drug habit last year, but it had given her the idea to take up this cause. He was one of the lucky ones and had come clean before it destroyed him. Seeing the effects of drug abuse first hand had shaken her to the core, and she had to do something about it. She knew now God must have a plan for her, and she was prepared to see it through, whatever it took.

5 Clues

"Page mark…"

Zac awoke, clutching his pillow. He'd heard the words as if someone had whispered in his ear, close enough for him to feel warm breath on his cheek. It had startled him awake, his heart rate jumping. He peered into the darkness, the only light a soft glow from his alarm clock, showing the time as 4:51 a.m. He sat up, trying to recall the fragmented visions of his dreams. A feeling of struggle came back to him, as though he was trying to run through thick mud, his legs and feet too heavy to move. He'd tried to yell, but his throat was filled. The sensation of being pulled down by unseen hands into deep water was the last thing he'd felt before the voice in his ear woke him up.

"This is crazy. Now I'm having nightmares."

He walked to the small refrigerator, poured a cold glass of water and downed it. The room was stifling, though he had two fans going. He picked up a pen from the cup on his kitchen table, which doubled as a desk, and wrote the two words on a notepad. He knew he wouldn't forget them, but somehow writing it down released them from the forefront of his mind.

"So, Drowning Girl, what do you want from me? And what page needs to be marked? Or is it already marked?"

Now he was talking to ghosts. A nervous laugh bubbled in his throat, because he couldn't take it all seriously. It must be the stress, making him imagine things. Maybe Amanda was right, and his imagination had taken over.

Today he would get the film back, and perhaps it would show something. Or not. Either way, it was keeping him busy, giving him something to obsess about other than his future. Or Amanda in her bikini.

He stumbled back to his bed, flopping on it with a loud sigh. He was glad he wasn't dealing with this alone. Having Amanda's help made it more fun, even if she did think he was a lunatic. He probably shouldn't be spending so much time with her, but he found himself missing her when she wasn't there.

Like now. His favorite fantasy involving her began, like an 8-millimeter movie in his head. He re-played the night she had told him she was a virgin, but in this version, he didn't back away and she didn't storm out. They made sweet, passionate love, and he was happy to teach her how to pleasure him, and to find out what pleased her. In his mind, she was beneath him, her head back, moaning in ecstasy.

In her absence he pleasured himself, but in his mind it was her hands upon him, her lips and tongue that drove him to the brink. He knew it was just a fantasy but instinct told him they would be so good in bed together. Their make out sessions had left him breathless—the woman could kiss, and she wasn't shy about it. It had taken all his will to put her aside that night, when she was begging him to take her.

It was that image, her begging him to plunge inside her softness, which threw him over the edge now. As his spasms subsided it was her face he saw. Dark copper eyes looking into his with love.

Love? Holy crap.

He rolled over and hugged his pillow, groaning. Now he had two women attempting to drive him crazy. One was a ghost, and the other was a red-headed, hot-blooded virgin who was out to get him, body and soul. He had a feeling he knew which one was going to succeed.

~*~

It was only her second week working part-time at the library, and Amanda was already bored. She enjoyed being around books, and had taken a stack home for her summer reading, but it was having to be so dang quiet all day that got on her nerves. When someone did talk to her, it was only to ask questions on how to find something or what to do about overdue book fines.

She'd set aside some books for Zac, all about ghost photography and ghost sightings. Apparently it was common for apparitions, or what might be mistaken for one, to show up in photos since photography was invented. Balls of light, or orbs, were the most common, and from what she'd gleaned from the captions no one had ever proven they were anything supernatural. It was usually found to be a trick of lighting, reflections bouncing off the camera lens. But she had to admit it was interesting to speculate on, especially the ones that took on almost human shapes.

"Good morning, Sunshine," Zac greeted her as he walked in, using his outside voice.

"Shhhh. Oooh, donuts."

She'd shushed him, but the box of donuts in one hand and coffee in the other made her forget the rules. She opened the wooden gate to allow him behind the counter, and he placed the food on a nearby table.

"I thought you might be hungry," he whispered.

"Thanks, I am. Hey, I found these for you, "she whispered back, handing him the four books she'd found.

"Cool. Thanks. I'll go read them now."

Looking up, she saw her supervisor, Miss Bankston, walking their way. "Go, you're not supposed to be back here. I go on break in a few minutes, I'll join you."

He made it to a nearby table before Miss Bankston spotted him. Several minutes later, Amanda sat down, peering over his shoulder at the notes he'd already written on a pad. He set his pen down, and stood up. "Can we go outside for a minute? I have to show you something."

His tone was casual, but her stomach flipped. He had a faraway look in his eyes, and she couldn't fathom what it meant. But then, to say he'd been acting strange lately would be an understatement.

They sat under a tree on the library lawn, the canopy of leaves providing a cool shade. The breeze ruffled his wavy hair, and his beard was unkempt as always, reminding her of a caveman, but a better looking one than she'd seen in any book. She stifled a giggle at the mental image of him dragging her by her hair, cave-man style, and asked, "What's up?"

"I've been having dreams about her, the ghost. Well, nightmares. I feel like I'm drowning, and I can't get away. Then last night, she actually talked to me."

"What'd she say?"

"Just two words. 'Page mark'."

Her worry for him increased tenfold. He really was taking this to heart. While she didn't believe it was real, it was affecting him, so all she could do was be supportive. "Hmmm. I wonder what that means. Do you have any idea?"

"No, but look at these."

He pulled an envelope from his backpack and handed it to her. She opened it to find a stack of photos, from the last time they went to the lake. On top was the one he'd taken of the bush where the Drowning Girl had supposedly appeared.

"It's an orb. I just read about these. It's quite common, due to light refraction."

He took the photo back. "I don't know what caused it, though. There was no sunlight to reflect off anything. It was about to rain, remember?"

"That's true…was this the birthday camera, or the disposable one?"

"The one you gave me. The vintage camera. I didn't use flash, so I still can't explain the discoloration there, right where she was standing. And this was less than a minute after I saw her."

He pointed to the photo, and she looked at it again. The "orb" was a small spot of light at the edge of the bush, but behind it were faint squiggly lines, barely visible, in the rough shape of a person.

"No. It can't be. This has to be some interference with the development of the film then, right?"

"I guess. Right now, I'm not sure what I believe. Look through the rest. Not one speck of light, no squiggly lines, just on that one, taken moments after she disappeared."

She leafed through the stack, and he was right. "Well, that's weird."

"Uh huh. Let's just say, for the sake of argument, that this is the ghost of a girl who drowned. How can we find out if anyone drowned on the lake, near that spot?"

"Shouldn't be too hard. I can look through the microfiche in the library for news articles or obits. If that doesn't turn up anything, maybe the ranger's office would know. Or my uncle."

He smiled, his first in a while. Her heart jumped a little.

"Well, I'm not anxious to talk to your Uncle Walt again, if I can help it. I still don't think he likes me."

She stood up, handing the envelope of photos back to him. "Aw, he intimidates everyone. It's his job."

They walked back to the library, agreeing to meet again at the pizza place Friday night to compare notes, unless something exciting came to light sooner. He checked out the books, and she watched him leave, with a mixture of curiosity and apprehension in her gut. She wasn't exactly intuitive, but she had a feeling something bad was going to happen if they dug into this.

But that wasn't going to stop her from standing by his side, ghost or no ghost.

6 Protests

She should have been home making dinner for her family like a good wife, but she knew they'd survive one night without her. She'd left a pot of spaghetti on the stove, and Victor could feed the boys for once. Tonight, Peggy Bresky had important work to do.

The M.A.I.D.s had assembled for their first protest, in front of a shop just off Main Street in the seedier section of downtown Fort Winston. What had once been a respectable family shoe store was now a tacky gift shop, specializing in items catering to illegal drug users.

"The dopers call it a 'head shop'. It's where they obtain drug paraphernalia," she explained to the group. Six faces stared back at her with disapproval, then conviction.

"Well, we certainly don't need this sort in Fort Winston, do we?" asked Bridget. "I would hate to see any of my students frequenting such a place. How are they even allowed to sell stuff like that?"

"We can't even look in the windows," Peggy pointed out, rapping her knuckles on the darkened glass. "They don't want casual passersby to know what they've got in there. And they sell their paraphernalia under the guise of being for use with tobacco."

The group murmured their disapproval again. She knew she was winding them up, but they understood so little and it was her job to educate them. Walt had been helpful in her education, even though she had learned of many things she wished she never knew existed.

Margo, the oldest of the group, made a face of disgust. "What a stupid name for a shop, too. 'Fort Dreamcloud'. That's what they want to turn this town into, I bet."

Peggy raised her sign up, holding it by the handle. "That is precisely why we are here, ladies. Let's get started."

They began to pace, single-file, up and down the sidewalk in front of the shop. It was just after five o'clock, and the street was filled with cars. Travelers on their way home from work or going to shops or restaurants for the evening were bound to notice them. Each woman held a sign with a slogan; Peggy's said, "Keep Ft. Winston drug-free". Others were a variation of that, so all who saw them would know their cause.

"Head shops must stop!" was their chant, and they shouted it in unison as they walked.

Cars honked as they sped by, and Peggy beamed. They were gathering attention. They kept pacing, staying close to the door, and blocked the path of a couple on the sidewalk. Both were long-haired and dressed like hippies in beaded shirts and fringed boots, and one of them almost knocked Margo over while trying to get in the door of the shop.

"Hey, watch it young man." Margo scolded, lashing out with her sign. She missed hitting him as they ducked inside the shop, the door slamming shut with a chime of bells.

"Can you smell that? That's incense," Peggy explained. "Druggies use it to cover the smell of marijuana and other putrid stuff."

Six noses sniffed the air, then wrinkled. They had so much to learn.

Resuming their chanting, they held the signs up high. Cars slowed down, drivers waved. Some noisy kids in a pickup truck yelled obscenities at them. But the M.A.I.D.s were on the job, and would not be swayed by a few hecklers.

The door bells chimed again and a man came out, wearing a tie-dyed tee shirt that appeared as though he'd slept in it for a week. His forehead was prominent due to a receding hair-line, but the rest of his hair was frizzy and past his shoulders. With his mutton-chop sideburns and slight overbite, he reminded Peggy of an overgrown walrus. His voice was gravelly, the voice of a chronic smoker.

"Hey, you can't do this here. Go protest somewhere else."

Peggy stood face to face with the man, though he towered over her by at least six inches. "We most certainly can, we're only on the sidewalk. We have a right to be here. This is still a free country, you know."

"Yes, Ma'am, it is. And that's why I can sell whatever the hell I want in my own damn store."

Margo piped up, her face going red. "You can sell whatever you want, Mister, but that doesn't make it right. That stuff entices kids to take drugs. You are catering to that, making it easier for them. You should be ashamed of yourself."

The rest of the ladies chimed in with agreement, and he looked around, shaking his head. "Aw, get with the twentieth century, man."

He disappeared inside his shop, and the ladies cheered. They took up their signs once more, waving to the cars, their enthusiasm for their cause renewed.

Peggy knew then she was doing the right thing. She vowed to do whatever it took to rid Fort Winston of the scourge that threatened the very fabric of their society. People like this store owner might think they were just a group of old-fashioned biddies. Maybe he was right, but she knew they had the power to make a difference.

Tonight her family was eating without her, but how proud would they be when she won an award for cleaning up Fort Winston? Or was asked to speak at a Mayor's luncheon? The future was wide open, and Peggy Bresky was ready to take it on.

~*~

Zac had barely finished his beer, when he ordered another. It was Friday night and the pizza place was filling in with families and groups of college kids. He'd considered calling Amanda and meeting somewhere else to go over their findings, but he was able to snag a booth in the back so they could have a little privacy. The beer was helping to calm him, though he couldn't explain his anxiety. He was hoping Amanda had found some logical explanation and he could put all this ghost nonsense to rest.

She came in with her usual bright smile, causing his heart to skip a beat. The sun had kissed her nose with a few new freckles, and her hair was undone, not in the usual pony tail she wore when it was hot. Her green tank top and denim wrap-around skirt hugged her curves, and he reminded himself he was not supposed to notice.

Yeah, right.

He stood up to greet her with a loose hug, then sat back and took a swig of beer to cool off. "So'd you find out anything?"

"Not much, I'm afraid. The microfiche must not be up to date. The articles I found about people who died on the lake were from several years ago. One was a small child, and two were older guys who had heart attacks. A lady died, too, but that was in one of the picnic areas, over by the marina."

"Ah, too bad."

Their food arrived, so they talked about other things while they ate. He'd ordered their favorite, pizza with pepperoni and pineapple, and they laughed about it just as they always did. "They still give me weird looks when I order our pizza," he said, taking another bite.

"You'd think they'd be used to it by now. We're the only weirdos who order this."

He nodded, more aware than ever how compatible they were. Little things they shared like this were comforting. He would surely miss her, when he had to leave.

"I had another dream about the ghost," he said, his voice low, looking around at the other tables. No one paid them any attention, so he kept going. "She was at the ledge, where we were that day I saw her. There was a campfire, and she was laughing, talking to someone. I couldn't see who was with her, 'cause it was dark. Then I heard her scream and I woke up."

"Wow. Does it scare you? It would creep me out, for sure."

If she thought he was crazy, or exaggerating, he couldn't tell. Her concern seemed genuine. "It did at first. But I'm getting used to it, I guess. Now I'm just curious as hell to find out what really happened, and who it happened to."

"Well, we could talk to Uncle Walt. Maybe he knows something."

"Yeah, but I doubt telling him we're getting clues from a ghost is the way to go."

She laughed, imagining her Uncle's face no doubt, upon hearing they were ghost-chasing. "I'm his favorite niece, I'll think of something."

Later they were in the parking lot, saying goodbye. He'd walked her to her car, parked in the far corner by a tree. Night was closing in, and the air was balmy with the lingering heat of the day.

He leaned up against the car next to hers as she threw her purse on the passenger seat of her Pinto. He couldn't resist teasing her. "I still don't know why you drive this gutless wonder around."

She jabbed his chest with a finger. "Hey, it's still roomier than your Beetle."

"Maybe. But at least mine has more than one speed."

The next thing he knew, she was hugging him tight. "Oh, Zac. Tell me you won't leave Fort Winston. I don't know what I'd do without you."

His arms came around her, and he struggled for something to say. "What...what brought this on? Did I say I was going anywhere?"

She looked up at him, a glisten of moisture in her eyes. He would never understand women—one minute they were laughing at you and the next, crying on your shoulder.

"Well, you said you would stay until you solved this Drowning Girl thing. But then what? I want to help you, but I really don't want you to leave once we figure this out. I'm sorry if that sounds selfish, but I can't pretend anymore."

He held her away from him so he could see her face. The anguish there surprised him. She always seemed so cool and easygoing, but he may have underestimated her feelings.

Feelings he shared but could not bring himself to admit. He just wasn't ready, and he didn't want to lead her on.

"Amanda, I...."

His words were smothered by her lips. It wasn't a friendly kiss, either. She'd thrown her arms about his neck, pulling him to her, the softness of her chest smashing into his. His brain reeled in protest but his body's response was the opposite; any passerby would have told them to get a room. His hands traveled of their own accord, one grabbed her hip while the other was buried in a handful of her hair. Their tongues were waging war, exploring in a frenzy, months of pent–up desire spiraling out of control. A small part of his brain pleaded for reason to return, but it was too late.

"Amanda?"

The sound of a woman's voice broke them apart, both gasping for air. He turned toward the sound to see a small woman, with short, reddish hair, holding two pizza boxes and standing at the back of Amanda's car.

"Mom? Wh-what are you doing here?"

He didn't bother to tell her it was obvious the woman was taking home pizza, because he was as disturbed as Amanda sounded to find her mother standing there, witness to their make out session in a parking lot.

"I'm getting pizza for your family's dinner. What are you doing?"

The woman was small in stature but her voice was commanding. Zac now understood what she had said before, that her mother, Peggy, could be fierce. He sensed that fierceness simmering under the woman's calm composure now.

Amanda ran a hand through her hair, straightened her clothes. *That won't help, hon. We're busted.*

"Mom, this is my friend, Zac. We were just saying good-bye."

"Nice to meet you, Ma'am."

As he said the words, he heard the faint, "Hmmmph," Peggy responded with, before she turned to walk to her car. Over her shoulder she called, "You'd best be home before this pizza cools, Mandy."

He watched as the woman's gold-colored station wagon left the lot, noting the tight grip the driver had had on the steering wheel. Amanda was watching, too, then let out a groan as the car turned the corner. "Arrrggh. She pisses me off so bad sometimes."

"She's just being a Mom. No one wants to find their daughter making out in a parking lot."

She was hugging him again. "No, I guess not. Now, where were we?"

"Uh, we were saying goodbye, remember?" He pulled away, and opened her car door. "I don't want to get you in any more trouble."

Her pout made him want to be the one to attack this time, but he resisted. When she was safely belted in her car seat, he leaned in the window and kissed her, gently but brief. She touched his cheek, then started her engine.

"I'll see if I can talk to Uncle Walt tomorrow. He's coming over for a cookout at my house."

It was all she said, before she left him standing in the parking lot, wondering what he was going to do about her. About them.

And about a certain ghost.

7 Messages

Amanda's hands were shaking as she reached for the door handle. It was time to take a stand. She was no longer a child, and her parents would have to accept that sooner or later. Her mother's attitude toward Zac was beyond rude, something he didn't deserve. Humiliation and anger had built, layer upon layer as she drove home, recalling all the times her mother had tried to control not only her behavior, but her mind. Now it was her heart at stake, and she'd had enough.

"Mandy, we got pizza, and ice cream for dessert."

Sam's excited voice greeted her as she walked in. Howie also smiled and waved but didn't speak, as his mouth was full of pizza. She waved back, her stomach lurching at the thought of another bite. Being full from scarfing pizza wasn't the only reason her stomach was in knots.

Walking to the kitchen, she faced the reason—her parents, who turned to look at her with stern faces. She wondered if they'd practiced on each other to make sure they looked suitably menacing. Her father, usually the quiet one who left most of the discipline to Peggy, had likely spent the past half hour hearing every detail of their encounter in the parking lot. His grimace was one of disappointment, and it cut Amanda more than she had expected it would.

"Daddy, I need to explain…"

"Kitten, I know you're old enough to be kissing boys, but you need to be more discreet…"

Peggy jumped in, her voice shrill. "No, she shouldn't be kissing anyone, especially a guy like that hippie she was with. You should have seen him, Vic. I'm appalled, and I won't have my daughter running around with that type."

Heat erupted on Amada's face, and she clutched her purse to avoid throwing it down in a fit. They just weren't getting the message. She took a breath and willed her voice to remain steady. To act like a child now would only confirm her mother's position, and this was one fight she was not going to lose.

She cleared her throat. "Mom, you know nothing about Zac Daley, and I've purposely avoided having you meet him. I knew you'd judge him by his appearance only, which isn't fair. He's the kindest, most generous *man* I have ever met."

She had emphasized the word 'man', but the point was lost on her parents, who were both shaking their heads. It was Peggy who spoke, while Victor stood by, arms folded across his barrel chest.

"I don't need to get to know him, and I don't give a crap what he's like. Because people who dress like that, all sloppy, who don't cut their hair or shave, are telling the world they don't care. They are lazy, rebellious, and nothing but trouble. Has he given you drugs?"

She couldn't resist rolling her eyes, though she knew it would provoke them. "No, of course not. How many times do I have to tell you, I know better than that?"

Her mother's eyes narrowed. Like a shark detecting blood in the water, she moved closer to Amanda, her tight lips forming a frown. "So, he does drugs, but you wouldn't do them with him?"

"No, I never said he does them. He doesn't even drink anything but an occasional beer."

Her father spoke now, his blue eyes showing fatigue. "Mandy, you aren't drinking beer with him, are you?"

She stamped her foot, causing her brothers to peer into the kitchen from the dining room table. "No. Why can't you just trust me? I don't have to tell you anything, you know. I'm twenty years old and it's none of your damn business who I hang around with or what I do."

She turned to stomp her way up to her room, leaving all four of them to stare after her, open-mouthed. She knew she'd lost it, but she no longer cared. They weren't listening anyway.

She'd almost made it to the top of the stairs when Peggy scrambled up after her. "Don't you dare speak to us like that, young lady. We have every right to know what you're doing, and who you're doing it with. As long as you are living under our roof, you will abide by our rules."

From the landing, she whirled to face her mother, her voice calm and deadly serious. "Maybe I need to find another roof, then."

With that she slammed the door to her room and latched it, leaning against the door and breathing deep. Her limbs were shaking, and hot tears filled her eyes. She'd never before stood up to them, let alone cussed at her parents.

What is happening to me?

~*~

The house was soothingly quiet at three fifteen in the morning. Peggy could hear the steady sound of Victor's snoring from upstairs, assuring her he still slept. It was an annoying sound at times, but she knew she'd miss it if something ever happened to him.

Padding to the kitchen on silent feet, she was grateful for the moonlight shining in the window above the sink. She wouldn't have to turn any lights on, but even so, she could find what she needed in the dark. Inside the pantry, she knelt with cup in hand, pouring a generous shot of vodka. She really needed this. Her nerves were just plain shattered after that spat with Mandy.

In the refrigerator she found a half-empty can of orange soda, and poured it into her cup. Swirling it around with her finger, she then took a long sip, the familiar warmth sinking into her bones almost immediately. She let out a long sigh and sat at the dining table, fidgeting with the fringe on a placemat.

"Goddamn hippies."

She had whispered the curse, then crossed herself. It wasn't like her to cuss, even when alone, but she had come to despise anyone and anything which reminded her of what she was fighting against. No matter what Mandy said, even if that dead-beat looking guy she was hanging around with was nice, people would judge him to be a low-life. No, it wasn't fair to judge a person only on looks, but that was the way of the world. Mandy would be judged in a bad way simply for being with him. Why couldn't she see that?

"The company we keep..." she whispered, downing the last of her cup.

"Mom?"

She turned toward the voice to see her daughter standing at the bottom of the stairs. Amanda hesitated, then walked toward the kitchen. "I'm thirsty. I hope you don't mind me drinking *your* water."

"Of course not."

She purposely said no more. Mandy would come to her senses, in time. A moment later, the girl stood in front of her, struggling to say something. Peggy remained quiet, still fingering the edge of the mat.

"Mom, I'm sorry I yelled and cussed," she said in a rush, twisting the belt of her robe. "It's just...I'm still going to be friends with Zac, that's all."

"Just friends?"

It was a loaded question, and she held back from asking the one question she really wanted an answer to—was her daughter still a virgin?

"Yes. That's all he wants to be. We don't ever kiss like that, what you saw. It just...happened. It probably won't again, anyway."

She noted the disappointment in her daughter's voice, and wondered what on earth was drawing her to this guy. But a truce was being offered, so she took it.

"I understand. You just need to be careful about who you're seen with and what you're doing. This is a small town and people talk, believe me. You need to focus on your studies, get your degree next year. Then you can worry about going on your own, and finding another roof."

In the dim, she saw her daughter's smile, and knew they had reached an understanding. Mandy leaned down to hug her and placed a kiss on her cheek. She patted the girl's arm as she pulled away.

"Mom, are you okay? What's that smell?"

Peggy cleared her throat and stood, taking her cup to the sink. "Just some cough medicine, to help me sleep. Goodnight, honey."

"G'night."

She stood at the sink until she heard Amanda's door close. She had won. Her daughter seemed to get her message, loud and clear. Feeling more settled, she rinsed her cup and placed it on a dish towel. One drink was enough for now.

~*~

It was three-thirty in the morning, and Zac still hadn't slept. Kissing Amanda had not been his idea, but now he could think of little else. He hadn't realized until she attacked him, how much he really wanted her.

He'd been fooling himself all these months, thinking they could forget what happened and still be friends. Once desire like theirs had taken hold, there were only two options—leave and never see or hear from her again, or take her to bed and ravish her until they were both exhausted and satisfied. There was no living in the middle, not without consequences.

He didn't know how long he could resist, if she kept pursuing him like she was. He knew if he did take her to bed, afterward they would have a lot to deal with. For one, it was obvious her mother didn't approve of him. The woman barely spoke, judging him openly. Looking him over as though he was a vagrant living behind a trash bin.

"Not that this room is much better," he whispered into the darkness. He really needed to get on with his life. He'd put in a job application at the local paper that day, but they'd given him the polite 'we'll let you know' line. He'd applied at a few other places over the past month, but had no interviews. It was obvious he was wasting time here in Fort Winston, and it was past the time to move on.

Rising from the bed, he poured himself a cup of water and stood sipping it, gazing out the window at the moon. A shaft of moonlight slanted in on the table, which he'd left strewn with newspapers and copies of his resume. He bent to pick up a felt marker which had fallen to the floor, and noticed something peculiar. "What the…"

His voice trailed off as his fingers traced the word, "Page" encircled on the newspaper with black marker. He didn't recall doing it, and the hair stood up on his neck when he saw three other words, in random places on the paper, also circled. He whispered them, one by one. "Mark…fish….gill."

The cup dropped to the floor, splashing his feet with water. He didn't care, just stared at the paper in the dim light of the moon. His eyes darted around the room. He seemed to be alone, but who the hell had marked up his papers?

Flicking on the light, he searched the room. If someone had been here while he was gone, surely they'd have taken something. But everything was as he'd left it that morning. His camera equipment and guitar were all he had that someone might want to steal, and they were untouched.

I'm losing it.

"What do you want from me?"

It was late at night to be yelling at the top of his lungs, but he couldn't stop himself. A dog barked from somewhere, but otherwise there was no answer. He'd show this to Amanda, the only other person who might understand. Someone, or something, was sending him messages. That was obvious, but it still made no sense.

It scared him, but at the same time, his gut told him there was no threat. Yet.

He turned out the light, leaving the papers as they were. He lay back on the bed, wanting nothing more than to sleep it off, and wake up to find it had been a crazy dream.

Because he knew if he didn't figure this one out soon, he'd have to leave the state just to get some peace of mind.

8 Information

Peggy opened the screen door to her backyard with one hand while balancing a pitcher of lemonade in the other. She made the rounds, filling the cups of several chatting guests. Their first cookout of the season was a success, if the smiling faces were any indication. She had been concerned that her extended family might resent her inviting the ladies from her M.A.I.D.s group and their families, but everyone seemed to not only be getting along, but had plenty to talk about.

Kids were running around, playing on the swing set and tossing a beach ball. A small group of teenagers sat under the shade of the elm tree, looking bored. One long picnic table was occupied by the ladies, and the men sat in semicircle of lawn chairs around radio, listening to a ball game. The Colorado summer sun came and went as clouds drifted by, punctuated now and then with a cooling breeze.

Perfect. I wonder when the Mayor will show? Hope he brings his son.

She wasn't sure whether Mayor Keswick actually would stop by, but she had extended the invitation hoping to meet him and make a good impression. Obtaining the support of influential people was crucial to their cause. She could always ask for a formal meeting at some point, but a backyard barbeque was a much more relaxed setting. Plus, she'd love for Mandy to meet the Mayor's handsome son, Greg, who had just graduated college and was home for the summer.

"Where is she, anyway?"

"Who?" her husband asked, flipping another burger on the grill. She filled his cup with the last of the lemonade, and handed it to him.

"I was wondering where Mandy went."

"I saw her follow Walter inside, a few minutes ago. These dogs are almost ready, but the burgers will take a little longer."

"Fine, I'll get the plates."

She entered the kitchen, but voices in the den caught her attention. Standing just outside the door to the den, she listened. It seemed Mandy was talking about her summer job.

"Yeah, it's okay. It's easy work at the library, but boring sometimes."

"Well, Mandy, that's how most jobs are. Even police work gets boring sometimes. But you have to do your job to the best of your ability, no matter what. That's the only way to get ahead in life."

"I know...at least I get to read books. I picked up a few already to read. Which reminds me of something I wanted to ask you."

"Well, make it quick, hon. I can smell those burgers, and it's making me hungry."

She let out a short laugh, but kept talking. "Well I read this book about local history, how they built the reservoir and all that. But it made me wonder about that old campground on the far side, which is closed now. I heard some kids saying they closed it because people got hurt jumping off the cliff into the water, but did someone actually die from that, too?"

As she peeked around the corner, Peggy could see her brother's face in profile, his skin reddened by the sun. He doted on his niece, and Peggy was glad he'd come back into their lives after a long estrangement. It was a sad fact that she and her older brother rarely saw eye to eye, but lately they seemed to have moved past that and bonded over their shared concern for protecting the community, and their own children in particular. Taking time to listen to Mandy's silly questions was an example of how far they'd come.

"I think there was one death, a young girl, about a year ago. But the families asked for privacy, so it wasn't reported as widely as something like that usually is. Long story short, I don't know much about it."

"Oh. Is there any way to find out what happened to her?"

Walt had stood, and turned to leave the room. Peggy slipped back into the kitchen, and began gathering up plates. She heard him answer Mandy's question as he neared the kitchen, with Mandy following.

"We have a police report, I'm sure. But why do you care, anyway?"

"I thought it was someone I knew, that's all. I'm surprised I didn't know about it."

"Well, I'll take a look-see next week, and let you know if I find anything. Right now, I'm in search of a burger and a beer."

Peggy handed him a plate as he passed through the kitchen. "Beer is in the cooler," she called as the screen door slammed behind him. She turned to her daughter, who was leaning against a chair, looking as though she'd seen a ghost.

"You okay, honey? I think you need to eat."

Peggy handed her a plate, not waiting for a response. She'd seen through the window Mayor Keswick and his family had just arrived in the backyard, so her daughter's strange behavior would have to wait.

"Mandy, come with me. There's someone I'd like you to meet."

~*~

Amanda sat at the table, staring at her plate. Eating was the last thing she felt like doing. That, and being sociable to the guy her mother had seated her next to. He was cute and all, but she had more important things on her mind at the moment.

Like finding out who died at Horse Tail reservoir last year, and why it had been kept a secret. And wrapping her mind around what Zac had told her that morning, that strange messages had appeared in his apartment, words circled on a newspaper by some unseen hand.

She believed him, though for the life of her, she didn't know why. She wouldn't have believed it if anyone else had told her about the strange things he was seeing and hearing. It had all started with that old camera she gave him, so she felt some responsibility in all that was happening, and it made sense in some weird way to believe him. And she had seen his photos of *something* in the lake....

"So, you go to FWU?"

Her thoughts were interrupted by the guy, Greg, her mother said his name was. His green eyes were focused on her, his smile was suggestive. If she wasn't involved with Zac, she might be interested. But disinterest was no reason to be impolite.

"Yeah. Senior next semester."

"Cool. I just graduated from State, in Denver. Poli-sci. Dad's idea, of course."

She liked his sardonic smile. She knew what it was like to bend to her parent's wishes most of the time, even if she didn't always agree.

"Congrats." She pointed to herself. "Liberal Arts. Still not sure what I want to do yet. But my parents are okay with that, for now."

She toyed with her food, taking a bite of the burger Peggy had assembled for her. Greg kept talking, but she was only half listening. She had to slip away and call Zac to tell him what Uncle Walt had said about the girl who drowned.

She finished most of her burger then stood. "Sorry, but I've got something to do. It was nice meeting you, Greg."

His face registered surprise, and he immediately began looking around for someone else to talk to. Apparently, he wasn't used to girls bailing on him. He had already stood to leave when he answered her.

"Sure. Catch you later, then."

She hurried into the house, aware of her mother's eyes on her. Two people she had disappointed just now. *Oh well.*

In her room on her pink princess phone, she sat waiting for Zac to pick up. When he did, he sounded groggy.

"Dang, it's four o'clock, Zac. You're sleeping in the middle of the day like an old man?"

"Hey, you try sharing a room with a ghost. Kinda keeps a person up at night. I'd still be sleeping if you hadn't called."

"Well, wake up, 'cause I have some news."

~*~

Peggy stood outside of Amanda's door, her hand poised to knock. Her daughter's voice was audible, and her tone excited, so she leaned her ear close to the door. She wouldn't normally eavesdrop, but something had caused Mandy to give the Mayor's son the brush off, and she wanted to know why.

"...No, he didn't give me a name, he couldn't remember. But a girl did die out there, and her family wanted it kept quiet for some reason."

There was a pause while Mandy waited for the other person to speak. Peggy had a feeling it was that Zac character, which pissed her off even more than Mandy's sudden disappearance. This obsession of hers was getting out of control.

"So you think maybe it was her ghost, sending you messages? Well, I admit that was weird about the newspaper, but..."

There was a long pause and Peggy strained to hear. Then Amanda made a 'pffft' sound, as though she didn't believe what the other person was saying.

"C'mon, Zac...are you sure you haven't been using that roach clip you found? Maybe you were high and don't remember writing that stuff."

Her stomach fluttered with nausea. *I knew it. That guy's doing drugs. Why does she keep lying to me?*

Mandy laughed. "Well, there has to be someone who knows what happened. I'll ask around, and keep pestering my Uncle. If you get any more strange messages, call me. I'll come spend the night with you so you won't get scared."

Her daughter laughed again, but Peggy was furious. Talking about ghosts and dead people was bad enough, but the drug references and indecent flirting was too much. It was clear Amanda wasn't being honest, just telling her parents what she thought they wanted to hear. She and that hippie were much more than *friends*.

Pounding on the door, she announced, "You'd better get back downstairs, young lady. You promised to help me with this cookout, not lounge in your room on the phone all afternoon."

The polite, 'Okay, Mom' through the door didn't ease her anger, but as she reached the kitchen, she pasted a smile on her face. Her public was waiting, and they looked to her for leadership. The fact that her daughter was heading toward trouble was her own burden, and one that she would be dealing with pretty damn quick.

9 Names

By ten p.m., the Cellar bar was packed, as it usually was on a Saturday night. Most of the regulars were there, except for the one person Zac was hoping to see—Wes Porter. He couldn't stand the guy personally, he had a rep for being a ladies' man, and a spoiled rich kid. He was vain, shallow and good looking, yet Wes seemed to be friends with just about everyone. So if anyone had information on the girl who drowned, Wes would be able to find out.

It was fifteen minutes later when Zac was bombarded with drink orders that he spotted Wes above the crowd. Tall and blond, he had a perpetually smug smile on his face, evident as he watched one of his buddies banging on a pinball machine. He laughed and downed his beer, heading to the bar. Zac finished the last order and hurried down to where Wes was standing.

The promise of a free beer was all Wes needed to hear. Zac told Leah, the other bartender, he needed a break and met Wes in the alley behind the bar.

Wes lit a cigarette, and laughed in a plume of smoke. "Hey man, thanks for the free beer. I thought you might still be mad at me for that spiked brownie thing last year."

Zac forced a grin, irritation close to the surface from the memory of his friend, Sarah, ingesting a drug-laced brownie unknowingly. But Wes had known. He just thought it would be funny to not tell her.

"Yeah, well, that wasn't cool, but it all worked out. Sarah survived okay."

He took another drag of his cigarette. "So what's up, then?"

"Know anything about a girl who died last year on Horse Tail?"

"I heard about it, yeah. Why?"

"A friend of mine thinks she knew the girl, wondered why it had been kept so quiet."

Wes leaned back against the wall, his face scrunched like he was trying to recall something. Zac had a growing feeling it was going to cost him more than one beer. He considered backing off, when the other man spoke.

"I don't know much about it, but I know who does. There's a girl who lives over on Silver Birch, who was a close friend of the girl who drowned. I can give you her number, but she may not want to talk about it."

"Great. I have a pen at the bar. Thanks."

Zac turned to go back inside, and Wes threw his cigarette on the ground, grinding it out with his foot. "And for another free beer, I can give you her name, too."

~*~

Amanda had agreed to meet with Zac at the park after church, thankfully at noon. He'd been up all night again, finally getting some sleep around dawn. Every time he fell asleep, he'd dreamed of either the Drowning Girl, or even worse—Gina. It felt good now to look at Amanda and see a pretty woman, alive and healthy.

She was dressed conservatively, but still looked sexy as hell to him. Her ruffled blouse was unbuttoned just so, her legs were bare under her skirt, and her hair fell in russet waves over her shoulders. He always had the sense with her of heat shimmering under the surface of her skin, like a dormant volcano threatening to erupt at any second. Volcanoes were destructive, as her passion surely would be for him, should he choose to unleash it.

He cleared his mind of the lustful thoughts to focus on the topic at hand. "Her name is Vicki Sanchez. I called the number Wes gave me but it's disconnected."

"Figures."

"But he told also me told me she drives an old VW bus, painted all weird colors. I bet we can find her house if we just drive down Silver Birch looking for her bus."

"Let's go then. I have to be home by two. Told my mom I was meeting a girlfriend for lunch, but I don't think she believed me."

Twenty minutes later, they rang the doorbell of an old house where Vicki Sanchez's purple VW bus was parked in all its glory. It was just as Wes had described, covered in pink flowers and yellow peace signs which looked like they had been painted on by a stoned chimpanzee. The thing reminded him of a certain popular cartoon about ghost-hunting teenagers and their goofy Great Dane. Suppressing a laugh, he knocked on the door.

It appeared that Vicki was not a morning person, answering the door in an old robe, with her hair a matted brown cloud around her head. Her bloodshot eyes looked them over, and thinking they were there to sell her something, she almost slammed the door. Zac grabbed it, causing her to stop and look at him in alarm.

"Wait—Vicki Sanchez, we need to talk to you." Dark almond-shaped eyes assessed them, and Zac thought she still might slam the door on his fingers, so he talked fast. "I was told by a mutual friend you might know something about the girl who died up at Horse Tail reservoir."

There. He had her attention. Either she'd talk to them or she wouldn't.

"What mutual friend?" Her voice was wary, but curiosity showed in her expression.

"Wes Porter. My friend Amanda and I just want to ask you some questions, if you don't mind."

She looked past them to the street, then glanced over her shoulder. "Are you guys cops?"

Amanda looked startled. "No, of course not. I think I might have known her and want to know what really happened to her."

This seemed to appease the girl, and she opened the door. "Come in, then."

It wasn't the friendliest of invitations, but at least she was willing to talk. They walked into the house, which smelled as though a window had never been opened. The drapes were drawn to block out the sun, giving the place a cave-like feel, and it appeared that dusting furniture was Vicki's least favorite activity. In her cluttered kitchen, she made them each a cup of herbal tea, and they sat at the table, which was piled high with boxes, bags, and newspapers. Apparently Miss Sanchez was also a packrat. She stood at the sink, dunking her teabag in and out of her cup, with an expression that verged on tears.

"Some days, I just miss her so much. There was no one else like Paige, and there never will be."

Amanda and Zac spoke at once. "Paige? That was her name?"

"Yes. She was my best friend since we were kids."

Staring at each other in silence, they let Vicki have her moment. She had let the tears come, wiping her eyes with a napkin. Amanda spoke first, her voice soft with sympathy. "I'm so sorry for your loss, Vicki. It must have been awful. It's okay if you don't want to talk about it, but we'd like to know what happened."

Vicki sniffed and took a sip of tea. She fidgeted with the belt of her robe, staring off into space. When she spoke, her voice was thick with emotion. "She was with her boyfriend at the time, up at the old campground that overlooks the lake. She didn't normally do drugs, but he persuaded her to smoke pot with him. She gave in, which was a grave mistake, because apparently it was laced with something bad and she kinda went crazy. At least that's his story, anyway. He said she jumped into the lake, though he told her not to. She hit the rocks and drowned."

Amanda shot him a look of bewilderment. Zac cleared his throat, hoping he sounded sincere, and not as freaked out as he was feeling. "That's horrible. I can totally understand why her family kept it quiet."

Vicki's face went sour. "Yeah, well...her folks won't even talk to me, or any of her friends anymore. They're very straight-laced. Wouldn't even let me go to the funeral, if you can believe that shit."

They both made sounds of consolation, shaking their heads. Vicki's account had played out in Zac's head like a movie, giving him an odd sensation of déjà vu. Now there was one more piece of information he needed. "So what did you say her boyfriend's name was?"

"I didn't. But his first name's Mark. I have no idea what his last name is. Paige was dating him for a while before she died, and we never saw her much. She was always with him."

The room seemed to be tilting for a moment, as his head spun with the information. *Paige and Mark. Holy crap.*

They stayed for another ten minutes, just to be polite. Vicki was more awake now, chatting about her friend and things they had done together. What really gripped Zac's heart was her revelation that she often had vivid dreams about Paige, too.

"It's like she's trying to tell me something important, but I don't know what."

Amanda's eyebrow went up at that. "Wow. That's strange, isn't it? If only there really was a way to communicate with her."

She looked at Zac, who felt his face grow warm. To his surprise, Vicki laughed. "Oh, but there is. You might think I'm crazy, but I'm going to tell you anyway. I'm having a sort of a séance tonight. I'm going to get her to talk to me once and for all."

This was turning from weird to downright insane. Zac looked in her eyes to find Vicki was serious. "How will that help? How will she be able to talk to you?"

"Easy. Have you ever used an Ouija board?"

~*~

As they headed back to the park to get Amanda's car, her brain was reeling with the fact that the messages Zac had been getting from the ghost had actually been verified. Vicki's account of what had happened to Paige left no doubt.

"How in the world is this possible, Zac? Maybe somewhere, you heard about Paige's drowning, and your subconscious is throwing it back to you?"

"I suppose that's possible, but why now? And it doesn't explain anything about the camera. My subconscious didn't put a drowning person in those photos."

She had to admit there was no way to explain the weird photos. "But you're the only one who actually saw her in the water and at the campground. I never did, even when I looked through the camera."

"Great, so I'm the chosen one. I'd have been happy to avoid all this, you know. And what about the words circled on the newspaper? There are still two words left that we haven't figured out."

"Well, now that we have their names, we can try to find out who they are. Maybe the other words aren't that important. I mean, 'fish' and 'gill' may have just been there to indicate the lake, right?"

Zac tapped his fingers on the steering wheel. "Maybe we'll find out more from Vicki tonight with her crazy Ouija board experiment."

Amanda laughed, more from nerves than amusement. "I've never tried one of those, have you? My Mom said that's the devil talking from those things. She would absolutely flip if she knew I was anywhere near one."

"Ahh, it's no big deal. There was one at a sleep over when I was a kid in Jersey. It seemed like it told us some creepy stuff, and a few kids got scared. But I never believed in it."

"And now? Now that you've actually seen and heard from a ghost?"

"We'll see, okay? In the meantime, can you try to find out the boyfriend's last name?"

As he talked, he was pulling at his goatee as he often did when faced with a problem. She wanted to grab hold of his goatee herself and kiss him hard, until her uneasy feeling went away. Instead, she fidgeted with her purse, playing with the leather fringe. "I'll go see Uncle Walt tomorrow morning. But what about tonight? Should I just meet you at Vicki's?"

He had pulled into the parking lot next to her car. As she got out, she heard him answer. "Yeah. I should be able to get off work a little early. I'll meet you there about quarter to ten."

She paused by his open window to squeeze his arm. "It's gonna be okay, Fuzzy. Guess I should have believed you from the start."

"That's right. You'll learn."

He took off, the VW engine buzzing. Now all she had to do was figure out how she was going to get out of the house that night without her mother wondering what she was up to. Telling Peggy she was going to séance party to use an Ouija board to talk to ghosts was out of the question, though she would love to see the expression on her face if she did.

10 Evidence

"Thanks so much for coming over on short notice, Peggy," Margo gushed, leading Peggy into her kitchen. "I've made a pitcher of lemonade, so help yourself while I go get it."

Peggy still didn't know what 'it' was, only that Margo had been quite upset at church that morning. Her grandson, Seth, had moved in with her recently, and while cleaning his room she found something which disturbed her, and she asked for help identifying what it was. She had whispered in Peggy's ear that morning, "I think it has something to do with *drugs.*"

They all think I'm the expert now. She didn't mind, even though she was still learning. It was tough keeping up with the lingo and behavior of kids these days, but she kept her ears open and her eyes peeled. You never knew what the next dangerous fad was going to be.

She poured the lemonade and sipped it, eyes wandering over the knickknacks cluttering Margo's kitchen. *So many cows.* Ceramic, plastic, wooden, all sizes and shapes of cow figurines perched on every shelf and along the counters. They stared at Peggy with amused bovine expressions, so she stared back.

"Here it is," Margo announced, placing a bundle on the table. It was a dishtowel wrapped around something, and Peggy poised her hand above it.

"May I?"

Margo nodded, her face etched with concern.

The object was made of amber-colored plastic, a tube about six inches high, set on a base. There was a small projectile on one side, and a tiny hole opposite. The projectile was made of metal, about an inch long, with a bowl-shaped end. The tube was open at the top, so Peggy sniffed it.

"Ew." She huffed out a breath. "It smells like old socks, musty."

Examining it, she noticed the tiny bowl was blackened inside, and she sniffed that. Residue of some kind was evident, and it came off on her finger as she touched the inside of the bowl.

"Well? What is it?" Margo stood over her, wringing her hands. She hated to give bad news, but there was no way to avoid it. Plus it was kinder to let the woman know what she was dealing with, so she could protect her grandson.

"It looks like some kind of smoking device, Margo. I'm sorry, but it looks like your grandson has been smoking dope."

She felt the anguish she saw on Margo's face deep in her own gut. It was a shame, the things a mother, and even a grandmother, must endure to keep their children safe. Margo's grandson would certainly be better off if this thing went missing. *Perhaps it could be useful in other ways...*

"What should I do? Will he get in trouble?"

Peggy set the object down on the table, and patted Margo's hand. "Don't worry. I'm going to find out for sure. I'll take this to Walter at the Sheriff's office and have them evaluate it. Then I'll let you know what it is, and what you should do."

"Thank you. I'm just so glad to know I'm not alone in this."

"Of course not. We M.A.I.D.'s. have to stick together, right?"

Ten minutes later she had the object wrapped in the towel, inside a brown paper bag and stashed under the back seat of her car. She felt a tinge of guilt at the plan forming in her mind, but it would solve a bunch of problems at once. If the timing worked out, she'd use it. If it didn't, then she'd carry on, and no one else had to know she'd even thought of it. But if the opportunity presented itself, she'd take that as a sign she should execute her plan.

Sometimes the ends justify the means, especially when you have a family to protect.

~*~

"Mom, I'll be staying over at Tess's tonight. We're going to watch that Beatles movie that's on T.V."

Peggy barely looked up from the newspaper she was reading. "Don't you have to work tomorrow, hon?"

Amanda slung her purse over her shoulder, prepared to walk out the door before too many questions were asked. "Not until ten. I'll be there on time. Don't worry."

She blew her mother a kiss and hurried out the door. Once in the car, she unbuttoned her shirt, tossing it in the back seat. Her low-cut tank top was more comfortable in the balmy heat, and was sure to catch Zac's attention. Tonight she had the perfect alibi, and was intent on finding a way to get him to take her home with him.

He can't resist forever. She fantasized as she drove across town, picturing how it would be to spend the night in his apartment. In his bed. She wanted him more than ever, and she knew he wanted her. Their kisses were laced with fire, and there was only one thing that was ever going to put that fire out.

Distracted, she took a wrong turn, and had to double back to look for Silver Birch Street. For a moment, she thought a car was following her, but it turned on a side street before she reached Vicki's house. She shook her head at her own foolishness. *Okay, now the thought of Ouija boards and ghosts is making me paranoid.*

She didn't see Zac's car on the street and she was early, so she parked a few houses away to wait for him. Still unsure about Vicki and her roommates, the idea of going into the house alone made her uncomfortable. They were probably partiers, judging from all of the rock posters on the walls and beads hanging everywhere. The faint scent of something stale and earthy had hung in the air, too, but Amanda couldn't tell if it was unwashed clothing or something else.

Like grass. I hope they don't smoke it around me. I just want to do the ghost stuff to help Zac, and get out of there.

What about Zac? If they offered, would he partake? He told her he went through a bad time when he first came to Colorado and had dabbled in drugs back then. He'd since gotten sober and gave it all up, but would be tempted? She'd never seen or suspected him of taking anything since they'd been hanging out, so she had to take him at his word that he wouldn't get high.

A voice at her side startled her, saying, "Hey. You ready?"

She let out a gasp, looking up to see Zac standing at her window. He helped her from the car, and they walked to the house. Vicki's brightly colored VW bus was still parked in the driveway, and they could hear music from inside, though the windows were closed. Two other cars were parked haphazardly on the lawn.

"Looks like this séance is gonna be quite a party," Zac remarked as he banged on the door with a fist.

Vicki opened the door and ushered them in. The room was darkened, lit only by candles and a blacklight, which caused everything to glow in odd colors. The cloying scent of incense was strong in the air, masking an earthy undertone. Loud music blared from three-foot tall speakers, and Vicki had to yell at them over Jimi Hendrix's wailing guitar.

"Ya want a drink? We got beer, and Jake brought a bottle of bourbon," she motioned to the kitchen. "We also have sodas if you're not into that."

They both accepted sodas from their hostess and were introduced to her roommates, Jake and Max. The crowd was a mixture of guys and girls—some were hanging about in the kitchen, and a few more in the living room. This wasn't exactly the atmosphere Amanda had pictured when Vicki invited them to come back for the séance; this was more of a house party than an exotic demonstration. It was bad enough to be doing something weird like using an Ouija board, but in front of all these strange people?

She was about to pull Zac aside to discuss her apprehension, when Vicki turned the music off and addressed the group.

"As most of you know, about a year ago I lost my best friend Paige. Her death was tragic, and I have been missing her terribly."

The room hushed, except for murmurs of sympathy. Vicki paused for effect, then continued in a softer voice. "I've been having dreams about her, and maybe I'm just grieving, but I've felt like she's been trying to tell me something for months. So I bought an Ouija board, and I'm going to use it tonight, to try to contact her."

Her friends offered encouragement, so she went about clearing the coffee table, explaining, "This will require concentration and no joking around. So if anyone doesn't want to participate or watch, feel free to use my room, or go hang out in the yard, until we're done. I'm really serious about this."

Max, Jake, and a few of the others decided to go outside, taking their beers and the bottle of bourbon with them. Amanda wondered how old they all were. She recognized a few from school, but had never met them before. *Oh well, not my business. Let's get this over with....*

They settled around the coffee table, where Vicki had placed the Ouija board. Two of the girls she didn't know, and one guy, sat in chairs nearby to watch. Vicki and Zac were on the sofa, and Amanda sat opposite them on the floor.

Zac looked at Amanda with a nervous glance, then spoke. "Uh, before we get started, there's something I think you should know."

Vicki's face was wary, but interested. "Okay?"

"This is gonna sound crazy, but I think your friend has been trying to contact me, too."

~*~

Peggy sat in the darkness, her eyes and ears alert. It had been fifteen minutes since her daughter and that hippie-freak walked into that house where some kind of party was going on. Lord only knew what Mandy was doing in there, and it was taking every ounce of patience she had not to bang on the door and demand her daughter leave.

But that would only make Mandy hate her, and cling to her freaky friends all the more. She trusted her daughter, but not the kids she was running with, especially *him.* Mandy would have to be shown he wasn't all she believed, as naïve and dreamy-eyed as she was around the young man.

Mandy had not seen her following in the family station wagon, but she'd had to turn down a side street to keep from being discovered. She hated resorting to subterfuge, but there was no other way. She'd even lied to Victor, telling him she'd gone to comfort Margo again tonight. But if she could make her daughter see the error of her ways before she got into real trouble, it would be worth the sacrifice and stress.

Reaching inside her purse, she found her flask. Taking a swig for courage, she waited while the familiar warmth settled in her stomach, soothing her nerves. She preferred a mixed drink to straight vodka, but it was easier this way. Replacing the flask in her purse, she pulled out a stick of minty chewing gum to mask the smell and kill the taste in her mouth. Then she reached under the back seat for the bag she had left there earlier.

Mandy's friend had parked a few cars behind hers. Peggy got out of her car, approaching the VW Beetle on silent sneakered feet. The street was deserted, no sound except faint music coming from the house Amanda had gone into.

She was pleased to find one of the back windows was rolled down a few inches. She'd been hoping the summer heat meant he'd leave one open, or a door unlocked. She emptied the contents of the brown paper bag into the backseat and hurried back to her car.

She waited, watching the house. A few minutes later some kids came out, two of them sitting on the hood of one of the cars, the others opening the door to the VW bus. They settled in, passing a bottle back and forth. One of them was lighting a cigarette, which they also began passing around, but they didn't hold it like a cigarette, between their fingers. Instead, they held it pinched between finger and thumb, inhaling deeply and holding it in.

"I'll be damned," Peggy whispered. *Unless I'm seriously mistaken, this is damned pot party, with underage drinking, too. What's next? An orgy in the mini-bus?*

"Jack pot."

Now all she had to do was find a pay phone.

11 Visitors

Zac sat still on Vicki's sofa, holding his breath. Her dark eyes stared back at him, her disbelief evident, but there was also a glimmer of hope. He didn't blame her, but he also didn't want to sound like he was making shit up if the Ouija board really did say something about Paige. When she didn't respond, he rushed to fill the silence.

"A few weeks ago, I was up at Horse Tail reservoir with Amanda," he nodded to her, and she nodded back. "I was trying out this vintage camera, just goofing around, and I thought I saw someone in the water right where your friend is supposed to have died. It looked like someone was drowning, but I could only see them through the camera lens. Every time I looked at the water directly, I saw nothing."

Vicki's expression had gone skeptical, but she just said, "That's freaky." So he continued, getting the words out before she could say anything else.

"Amanda didn't see her, or him, or whatever it was, through the camera, so we went to the ranger's office to alert them just in case. Later it turned out they hadn't seen anyone in trouble, so I figured it was a fluke. But when I got the photos back from being developed, they did show someone or something in the water. So next we went to the old closed campground on the other side of the lake, and while we were there taking more photos, I saw a girl standing by a bush for just a split second. I think it was her ghost, because she looked all banged up and wet, and disappeared as soon as I looked away."

There were gasps and muttering from the others in the room, but Vicki was close to tears. "She was there the night she died. She and Mark were at that campground."

Zac reached into his pocket. "And we found this in the dirt. I don't know if was his or not."

He handed Vicki the leather key tag with the roach clip attached. She turned it over in her hand, reading the letters aloud. "'M. F.' Yeah, it might be his."

"Well, it gets weirder. I've been having dreams about her, and I kept hearing the words, 'Page' and 'Mark', but I didn't know what they meant until we came here and talked to you."

She handed the clip back, and he stuck it in his pocket. He didn't bother to tell her about the words mysteriously circled on the newspaper, because he was still freaked out by that and it didn't look like Vicki needed much more convincing. She placed the Ouija board on her lap, turning to face him, and positioned the pointer in the center. "I don't know why, but she's using you to communicate. Let's see if we can get her to talk to us now."

"Oaky. It's been years since I used one of these things. I think I was like, ten," he laughed, still feeling a little freaky himself.

"Just put your fingers lightly on the planchette, don't push down," Vicki instructed, doing the same. She sat up straight, and took a deep breath. "We should try to relax."

He glanced over at Amanda, who was watching with a mixture of emotions on her face. Awe with a side-order of skepticism was how he'd describe it to her later, when they had a good laugh about it.

For a minute, nothing happened. The only sound was the occupants of the room breathing, waiting, and the occasional sound of laughter from the kids gathered outside in the driveway. He studied the board, it was the same design as the one he'd used as a child. A tan background with black Gothicstyle writing, the letters of the alphabet displayed in two semicircular rows, with a moon in one corner and a sun in the other, both with creepy faces drawn on them. Numbers one through 9, the words, "Hello" and "Goodbye", "Yes" and "No", and in the bottom corners, rough drawings of someone conjuring up spirits.

Zac tried to relax, but the suspense was palpable. *What the hell am I doing here? I really need to learn to mind my own business.*

He felt a tugging, and the planchette began to move. He looked up at Vicki, whose eyes went wide as she shook her head as if to say, "It's not me."

The planchette was only a few inches wide, shaped like a large teardrop, with a clear plastic circle in its center. In the middle of the circle was a metal pointer hanging down. What he remembered from years before was the tip of the planchette was what you watched, as the "spirits" or whatever it was, used it to spell out the words to communicate.

But now it was just sliding this way and that, taking his and Vicki's fingers along for the ride. It was an uncanny feeling, not moving the object, but being moved by it. He didn't get the sense that Vicki was pushing it, either. If that was so, he would feel some resistance. But this just seemed to flow, gliding their hands across the board.

Then it stopped, on the letter "Y". His eyes met Vicki's and then looked down as the planchette moved again to another letter, "O". By the third letter, they were both reading it aloud, "U".

"You!" Vicki gasped. "She's talking. I know it's her."

The message continued, and when the planchette stopped altogether, Zac repeated it. "You must tell him."

Silence filled the room, and Zac's gut turned to ice. *This can't be happening. It has to be our imaginations playing tricks....*

Vicki was tearing up again. Their hands were still resting on the planchette, and she stared at the board. In a wavering voice she asked, "Paige, is that you?"

The planchette moved, stopping just short of the word, "Yes" which was printed at the top of the board.

Tears slid down Vicki's cheeks, but he knew they couldn't stop now. "It'll be okay," he said, to comfort her and to calm himself. "Let's let her speak."

"Tell who, Paige? Tell him what?"

The planchette moved more easily now, as though Paige was gaining strength. It spelled out the word, "Mark", followed by "Not... his...fault".

"Her death is not his fault?" Amanda asked, now on her knees, watching the board closely.

"To hell it's not," Vicki muttered, and the planchette moved quickly, and with force to the word, "No."

They all sat stunned. Zac had removed his fingers, and Vicki had her head in her hands. When she looked up, her eyes were red, her lips quivering. "This is too much. I thought I was ready, but…"

Zac placed his fingers back in position. "Just one more question, please? Then we'll stop if you want. I need to know his last name."

Vicki wiped her eyes with the back of her hand, and moved her fingers back to the planchette. Immediately, it moved, spelling out the words, "Sorry, Icky".

Vicki burst out laughing. "That's what she used to call me, 'Icky'. And I called her 'Pudge'."

The planchette moved back to "Yes", and then to the smiling sun-face. Vicki laughed again, and told Zac to ask his question.

"What is Mark's last name, so we can find him?"

The planchette moved from one letter to another, everyone watching and repeating the letters out loud. When the movement stopped, Amanda said, "Fitzgill?"

Her eyes held recognition, and he felt a chill that raised the hair on his arms. *Crap. Fitzgill, not "Fish Gill". I don't freaking believe this…*

"That does sound familiar," Vicki said, her fingers still on the planchette. Zac had removed his, but it started moving again, only Vicki along for the ride.

"What's it saying now?" he asked, not sure if he should jump in or leave her to do it alone.

Vicki answered, "Get…out…now…?"

"Get out of here?"

The loud "whoop" of a police siren sounded just outside, and they looked up to see blinking red lights in the driveway.

"Shit." Vicki had tossed the Ouija board aside and ran for her bedroom. Seconds later, they heard the sound of a flushing toilet. Voices were loud outside, and Zac peeked through the window to see a Sheriff's car at the curb, and two uniformed deputies emerging.

"Crap," he whispered to Amanda, who was standing next to him. "This is not going to end well."

For the second time that night, he wished with all his heart he had minded his own damned business.

~*~

Amanda grabbed up her purse, unsure of what to do. Running out the back door didn't seem like an option, and she wasn't even sure she was in any danger.

"They can't do anything to us, can they?" she hissed in Zac's ear. He was standing next to her, peering out the window at the scene in the driveway. The deputies were holding flashlights, looking in the mini-bus through the opened door.

"I doubt it. I don't have any drugs on me, do you?"

"Of course not."

She watched as the deputies searched both vehicles in the driveway, then patted down Jake, Max, and the other boy who was with them. They had the two girls open their purses to be searched, and coming up empty, they walked toward the house. Just then, a second sheriff's car pulled up, and Amanda gasped as the burly figure of her uncle emerged.

"Oh, shit. It's Uncle Walt."

Vicki's voice behind her was shrill. "You're related to these guys? Is that why they're here?"

Amanda whirled to face her. "No, I have no idea why they're here."

The deputies were banging on the door. Vicki crossed to let them in, her face pink with anger. She shot a nasty look at Amanda and Zac, and faced the deputies, her head held high.

"Come in, gentlemen. We were just having a fun little séance. Glad you could join us."

The Ouija board still lay on the floor, and the deputies eyed it for a moment, then began walking around as though they owned the place. Amanda had always respected her uncle and knew his work was often dangerous, but the attitude his employees had now made her want to scream. Her new friends weren't hurting anyone, and nothing she had seen tonight called for the intimidating attitude she felt emanating from the deputies. When her uncle walked in behind them, she had to bite her tongue to keep from calling them out on it.

"Find anything yet, boys?" he addressed his deputies, who were searching the other rooms. Everyone else stood still, not speaking a word. Walter looked at Amanda, acknowledgment in his eyes, but he said nothing to her. The deputies returned, shaking their heads.

Amanda knew little about the drugs these kids may have had, and she really didn't want to know. Now that she and Zac had what they came for, she just wanted to get out of there. "So, can we go now? It's getting late," she prompted, looking straight at her uncle. His pale blue eyes looked back at her, then around the room.

"Once I'm satisfied, then you can go. Tripp, have you searched the vehicles?"

The taller of the two deputies answered. "Just the ones in the driveway, sir. We found an empty whiskey bottle, but no contraband."

Walter looked at Zac. Recognition showed in his eyes, and Amanda knew he must recall how Zac had helped him solve a crime last year. That had to count for something.

"Where's your car, young man?"

"It's on the street. Why?"

Walter nodded to his deputies. "Go search his vehicle. Give me the keys, son."

He held out his hand, and Zac frowned. She knew he had nothing to hide, and this was bordering on harassment. They had no evidence, no cause to suspect him of anything illegal, any more than they did to suspect her.

"My car is there, too. The Pinto. Here, while you're at it. *Sheriff.*"

She held out her keys, but Walter ignored her. She followed Zac out the door on the heels of Walter and the deputies. When they reached Zac's car, she glanced back to see Vicki and her roommates standing on the porch, watching. Her heart was pounding in her chest, but she didn't know why. Zac said they had nothing to worry about, and later she would talk to Walter and let him know just how she felt about this ridiculous scene.

The deputies had just opened the doors to Zac's car when the tall one said, "Here's something, sir."

He held up an object, a tubular, plastic-looking thing. He sniffed it, and ran a finger along the edge of it. "Looks like residue here."

He handed the object to Walter, who examined it, placing it to his nose. Then he nodded at Zac. "Check his pockets."

"Arms up," the taller deputy commanded, and Zac complied. He was thoroughly patted down, and Amanda gasped as something was pulled from his jeans pocket.

That damn roach clip thingy.

Walter frowned, avoiding Amanda's eyes. "Take him in for questioning, and we'll get a better look at this stuff."

"None of it is mine, I swear. I found that clip on the ground, and I've never seen that other thing before," Zac protested, but they already had the handcuffs out, and spun him around to clip them in place.

12 Revelations

Amanda watched as Zac was pushed into the back of the patrol car. She turned to her uncle, grabbing the sleeve of his uniform. "You can't do this. I know that wasn't his. I've never seen him do any drugs, or even talk about it. There's some mistake."

Walter looked down at her, and removed her hand, patting it. "Well, sometimes people aren't always truthful, are they? You'd best get home, your Mama's worried about you, I'm sure. I don't know why you were hanging around with this bunch, Mandy. They'll get you in trouble, sooner or later."

He glared up at Vicki and the other kids still standing on the porch. As he walked to his car, they scrambled back into the house, leaving Amanda alone on the sidewalk.

After everyone left, she sat for a few minutes in her Pinto, still stunned at the turn of events. She couldn't even be excited about witnessing real communications with a ghost, or think about what they were going to do now they had the name of Paige's boyfriend. With Zac being taken to jail, she had no choice but to wait and see what happened to him.

"That thing they found can't be his," she whispered, turning the key in the ignition. Something about the way the evening played out just didn't feel right. Why had the cops shown up at all? And why had Uncle Walt been there? If the deputies had just been driving by and saw the kids in the driveway, Walter wouldn't have arrived so soon. They wouldn't have called him in as backup for something like that.

Is it because I was here? Who knew I was here?

Mom. She must have followed me. She called the cops.

"Son of a screwed up gun. I should have figured she'd do something like this."

The car behind her that had veered away when she slowed down during her search for Vicki's house was no coincidence.

It was her own mother, tracking her down like she was some sort of criminal. She gripped the steering wheel and punched the gas pedal with her foot.

Though it was almost midnight, she drove as fast as her Pinto could go, which was just above the speed limit. Her thoughts built one upon the other, until she was shaking with rage. The tinge of guilt she felt for lying to her mother about where she'd been was smothered under her indignation at being spied on and speculation of how the plastic thing—*what was it called? A bong?*— wound up in Zac's car.

When she pulled in her driveway, she parked behind her mother's station wagon. On her way to the door, she placed her hand on the hood of her mother's car. *Still warm.* The living room was lit with a single lamp, and she entered to find Peggy at the dining table as though she'd been expecting her.

"Good. You're up," Amanda snarled, unable to retain her composure. "Are you going to tell me how Uncle Walt knew where I was tonight?"

Her mother stared back at her, lips pursed in defiance. "And just where were you, huh? Not where you told me you would be."

"So you followed me. I wasn't doing anything wrong, so it doesn't matter where I went."

Peggy stood, so they were face to face. She was a few inches shorter than Amanda, but it was clear from her stance she wasn't going to back down. "Yes, it does matter. First, you lied to me, and second, you were hanging out with a bad crowd. If you weren't 'doing anything wrong', then what *were* you doing there?"

I can't tell her the truth. She'll really flip out.

"Just hanging out, Mom. Even if other people drink or do drugs, I won't, so stop trying to police my every move."

"Don't you understand you can get in trouble, just by being around them? Don't you care how it looks?"

"Is that all you care about, how it looks to other people? I don't give a crap about that, honestly. You're just worried about what they'll think of *you* if I get in trouble."

She'd seen Peggy angry, plenty of times. But now a nerve had been hit, and her mother's face was contorted, as though she fought to keep from screaming. As Amanda stood only inches away, she noticed the redness of her mother's eyes, and a familiar sour, acidic smell reached her nose.

I've smelled that before, late at night...

"Mom, have you been drinking? Alcohol, I mean?"

Peggy's bloodshot eyes opened wide, her mouth hung open. When she found her voice, it was quivering, and Amanda couldn't tell if the slur of her mother's words was from anger or alcohol-induced.

"How dare you accuse me of something like that? I'm so mad, I can't even look at you now." She moved to leave. "I'm going to bed, and we'll discuss this in the morning."

Surprising herself, Amanda blocked Peggy's exit. "Oh no. Not until you tell me what you know about the thing they found in Zac's car."

Her mother shook her head, almost frantically. "I don't know what you're talking about. I don't even know what kind of car your friend drives."

This is crazy. Who else would have done it? Was it really Zac's? That would mean he lied....

Something in her snapped and she started to cry. It was all too confusing. What she had hoped would be her best night ever had turned into a nightmare, and she no longer knew who to trust.

Peggy's arms came around her. "Shh, Mandy...It's going to be okay."

She stiffened, but Peggy held her tight. Confusion and exhaustion had pushed her to the brink, so she buried her face in her mother's neck and let the tears flow. But that odd scent lingered, and she knew her mother wasn't the all-knowing, pure-hearted being she once believed. Peggy Bresky had secrets.

She also knew she wouldn't rest until she knew the truth about Zac. She had no choice, she had to know what kind of man he really was, if he was worthy of her love as she believed him to be. She also needed to know if he was ever going to love her back.

~*~

Zac hadn't been formally charged with anything, yet at two in the morning he was still sitting in a locked room at the police station. One of the deputies informed him he was being held in custody until a decision was reached about the object they found in his car. His hands were no longer cuffed, and they gave him some coffee and a stale donut, so he couldn't say he'd been mistreated. But it was ludicrous that he was even here in the first place.

Should've locked the damned car. He wondered for the fifteenth time that night how the bong ended up in his back seat. He hadn't touched one of those things in years. Maybe one of Vicki's friends saw the cops arriving and threw it in his car to hide it. It was the only possible scenario that made any sense. He couldn't imagine who might want to frame him. The only saving grace was there had been no marijuana to go along with it, or he'd really be locked up and in a worse mess than he was now.

He'd lost hope that Amanda might persuade her uncle to intervene. In fact, it was kind of weird how the good Sheriff had shown up when he did, as though he knew what was going down. He didn't think Sheriff Jackson frequently followed his deputies around as they patrolled the town at night, breaking up parties. Especially on a Sunday night, just before a holiday.

The effects of the coffee wore off, and he lay his head on his arms, leaning on the table. His body was drowsy with fatigue, but his mind still raced. The Drowning Girl's ghost had actually spoken through the Ouija board that night, which was the freakiest thing that had ever happened to him. If he hadn't been there to witness it, he'd never believe such a thing was possible. Now all he had to do, once he was out of this stupid mess, was find Mark Fitzgill. In his heart, he knew he'd never rest until he delivered Paige's message. He didn't understand why, but she had contacted him for a reason. Maybe once he delivered the message, he'd figure it out.

He wondered how Amanda felt about what they saw and heard. She must be as freaked out as he was. He hoped that maybe she'd come by in the morning to persuade them to release him. She was the only one who believed in him, unconditionally, and he didn't understand that, either. He wasn't her type, wasn't the kind of man to give her the life and love she deserved, but still she stood by him.

When he lifted his head again, it was throbbing. He'd fallen asleep, despite his efforts to stay awake. There were sounds of activity outside the door, so he looked at his watch. *Almost seven in the morning, crap. They have to let me out of here soon.*

The door swung open, and another deputy, one he hadn't seen before, handed him his driver's license. "You're free to go, Mr. Daley. Not enough evidence to hold you any longer."

Zac stood, stretching. "Thanks, but…I still have no idea how that thing got in my car."

The deputy held the door open, motioning for Zac to leave. "Neither do we, but the owner of the item called us with some more information. We're holding it pending further investigation, so yeah…you can go."

"Say no more."

He was out on the street in minutes, and began the long walk back to Vicki Sanchez's house to get his car. It felt good to be free, and he had a hell of a lot to think about.

~*~

Amanda woke up the next morning after a restless, fragmented sleep. The sun peeked in through her curtains, warming the room despite the small fan on her dresser. She'd lain awake most of the night, unable to get the image of Zac sitting in a jail cell out of her mind. The possibility that he had lied to her as her mother and uncle suggested gnawed at her, but she just couldn't bring herself to believe it.

She rose from her bed and stretched. As she came into the hallway, she heard the faint sound of the television in the den, indicating her brothers were watching cartoons. She paused outside her parent's bedroom door and listened. The sound of running water indicated her mother was in the shower, so she cracked the door open and slipped inside.

The closet door was ajar. With an ear toward the bathroom, she crept into the closet and found her mother's purse on the floor. She slipped her hand inside, her heart pounding in her chest. She'd never done anything as low as snooping, but she had to be sure. As she felt around, her fingers touched something smooth and metal. Pulling it out, she held the small canister in her hand, then opened the cap. She sniffed it, her worst fears confirmed.

Some kind of alcohol, all right. Mom, why?

The sound of running water stopped and she screwed the cap back, but it didn't go on easily. There was no time left, so she placed it back in the purse and left it on the floor. She exited the room to the sound of the bathroom door opening.

As she reached the kitchen downstairs, the phone rang. The sound of her uncle's voice on the line gave her hope. "Uncle Walt, please tell me you've released Zac."

"Actually, Mandy, your friend has been released, about an hour ago, but that's not why I called. I need to speak to your mom."

She let out a breath, her limbs going loose. He was safe. "Okay, I'll get her. Hang on."

When her mother picked up the bedroom phone, Amanda held down the button to hang up, then released it, placing her hand over the mouthpiece so she could listen undetected. She had a feeling Walter might mention Zac, and she had to know what was really going on.

~*~

Peggy picked up the phone, surprised to hear her brother's voice. He didn't usually call so early in the morning. "We had a strange call this morning, Peg. Seems a friend of yours thought we had something here that belonged to her. Or, to her grandson, to be exact."

Her stomach fluttered a moment. *No proof of anything.* "Oh? What friend? What are you talking about?"

"Margo Andrews. Said she gave you a drug-related item to bring to us for evaluation, and since she hadn't heard back from you, she called here. She was quite anxious to find out what it was."

The phone cord twisted in her fingers, but her voice was cool. "Oh, that. I think it's still in my car. I must have forgotten about it."

"No, it's not in your car, because we have it here. Found it in the backseat of that guy Mandy's been hanging around with, when we busted up that little party she was at last night. The one you gave us the heads up on."

Sweat formed at her hairline, just under her shower cap. He still had no proof she'd done anything, and if the outcome was getting Mandy away from that crowd, she'd do it again in a heartbeat.

"And a damn good thing I did, too. Maybe the one you found in his car did belong to him, 'cause it can't be Margo's grandson's. I'll go check my car, Walt."

"Well, let me know if you do find it, because we took the young man's word it wasn't his, after your friend called us. He had no actual drugs on him, or in his car, so we released him."

"Oh...well, what should I tell Margo?"

"She's on her way down here to identify it. But if you find anything else, let me know."

"Will do. I have to run now, Walt. I just got out of the shower."

His voice had been gruff, and business-like, but it softened a bit. "Okay. But how's Mandy doing?"

"She'll be fine. She was upset last night, but we came to an understanding. I don't think we'll have to worry about her seeing that Zac character any longer."

She heard a soft click, then Walt's voice again. "She's a grown woman now, Peg. You can't shelter her forever, though Lord knows, I understand why you'd want to."

By the time Peggy had dressed and gone downstairs to fix breakfast for the boys, Amanda had left for work. She could have used her daughter's help to prepare for the next day's 4th of July rally, but she'd make do. "Okay boys, after breakfast, we're making posters for the rally tomorrow."

She ignored their groans and poured cereal into their bowls.

13 Lovers

Amanda had only been at work for an hour, when she asked Miss Bankston if she could leave. "I'm really not feeling well. Must've been something I ate. I'll make it up on Wednesday, if you need me to."

Her supervisor's voice dripped with concern, but her frown told Amanda she wasn't happy. "Go on, then. I can handle it. And do feel better soon."

Once out door, she hurried to her car. A numb, dull feeling had replaced her earlier anger. She was still stunned at the lengths her mother had gone to, just to keep her from seeing Zac—following her, spying on them…not to mention calling the cops. Neither she nor Zac deserved such treatment. They hadn't done anything wrong.

But worst of all was the sadness that had seeped into her heart. *Why doesn't she like him? She never even gave him a chance.*

And Uncle Walt had been in on it, too, just as she'd suspected. She knew it was odd, him showing up at Vicki's house like that. Now she didn't know who she could trust.

Except for Zac. No matter how much they tried to turn her from him, she knew in her heart he was a good man. She'd been to his room a few times before, but this time, she could not get there fast enough. Fighting back tears, and emotions she was trying to suppress, she told herself to be calm. Her instinct to believe Zac was the man she thought him to be was stronger than her fears. She had to know once and for all, if there was any chance for them to be together. If she was going to defy her parents in order to be with him, she had to know he would support her decision to do so. Otherwise, she'd end up heartbroken, rejected by him and her family.

It was time for both of them to face the truth, and either be together or say goodbye, forever.

~*~

It was late in the morning by the time Zac reached his room. Stripping off his clothes, he collapsed on the bed in only his boxers. He was anxious to see Amanda, and discuss what had happened, but she was at work until three. He figured he'd catch a few hours' sleep, then find her before she left the library for home.

It felt good to be in his own bed. He settled into his pillow and the heaviness in his eyes began to tug him down into oblivion. A time later, he opened his eyes, thinking hours must have passed; but the digital clock showed only minutes. Soon he fell into a deep slumber, his body still but his mind whirling with fragmented images and dreams.

In his dream, he was driving, and on the passenger seat next to him was Gina, sleeping peacefully. She rested against her arm, which was curled under her head as she leaned on the window of the passenger door. Dark curls fell across her face but he still saw the wisp of a smile as she slept, perhaps dreaming of their new life together when they reached Fort Winston.

It had taken them days to drive from their home in New Jersey, but they were almost there. Denver had been a welcome sight, a respite from the endless ribbon of asphalt bordered by wide, open fields. But they had taken too long, looking at the sights, eating a good meal, even shopping in some quaint little shops. She'd been so excited, and he hated to cut their adventure short, so he indulged her. Now they were way behind schedule, and he was trying to make it up and get them to Fort Winston before midnight.

Road fatigue had set in, and he struggled to keep his eyes open. There was no traffic, no billboards, nothing to distract his eyes from the blacktop of the road. The radio wasn't much help; country stations drifted in and out, chased by soft static. It began to rain, and he counted the turns of his windshield wipers, determined to stay awake.

A jolt made him start, and his breath blew out in a whoosh as the car smashed into something. They had drifted off the road and into a telephone pole, the impact causing the car to twist and turn in circles. Gina screamed as the vehicle careened, then flipped over into a ditch, her voice drowned out by the sickening whine of the tires on the wet pavement, the crunch of metal and glass.

When the world stopped spinning, he opened his eyes. The car was on its side, with his door facing up to the sky. The only sound he heard was the patter of rain, and the rattle of his own breathing. The impact had knocked the wind out of him, and his shoulder was throbbing. But he was alive.

He turned to Gina to find her unconscious. Her head was titled at an odd angle, and his blood began to rush in his ears. He called out her name, and reached for her, but she didn't respond, her body limp. Blood trickled from her mouth, matting in her curls. He struggled out of his safety belt, and took her in his arms.

He cried more tears that night than he ever had in his life. He couldn't revive her, he knew she was gone. And it was his fault. They could have spent the night in Denver, but he'd been determined to get to Fort Winston. It was where they would start a new chapter in their young lives. They would take classes together, find jobs, get their own apartment. He was going to ask her to marry him on Christmas Eve, which was also her birthday.

None of that mattered now. He tried the door handle, but it was jammed. He had to get out, to get help. He pushed on the door, but it didn't budge. In a frustrated rage, he pounded on the window, trying to break it. He leaned back and kicked the door, over and over.

He stopped kicking, but could still hear the pounding, hear a voice, calling his name....

"Zac, it's me. Let me in."

His eyes flew open and he was not in the car with Gina, but in his own bed, and someone was pounding on his door.

Amanda was pounding on his door.

The moment he saw her, she fell into his arms. He was still dressed only in his boxers, and her frantic pleas to open the door had made him forget about putting on a shirt. Feeling her warmth next to his bare skin, only thin cotton separating his groin from her body, brought him fully awake. He held her at arm's length to look at her face.

"Hey, what's wrong? Why are you crying?"

She wiped her eyes with the back of her hand, and sniffed. "I'm so sorry you ended up in jail. So they didn't they charge you with anything?"

He closed the door, and guided her to the bed, the only place to sit, since the chairs near the small kitchen were piled high with books, papers, and photos. Handing her a tissue, he explained, "No. I wasn't even in a cell. Just a locked room. They questioned me for about a half hour then left me there all night, but it could have been worse."

"Well, it shouldn't have happened at all. My mom did it, Zac. She planted that bong in your backseat, then called Uncle Walt to break up what she thought was a wild party. Which means she followed me and will do anything to keep me from seeing you."

He didn't know what to say to her; it wasn't his place to advise her about her parents. It pissed him off that her mother tried to set him up, but he was more concerned with how Amada was feeling. In the end, no real harm had come from it, and he just wanted to comfort her. "Well, it doesn't matter now. Apparently it belonged to someone else, and they called the station looking for it. Which I thought was pretty weird."

Her confused look almost made him laugh, but he simply raised his eyebrows and shook his head. Then she laughed. "Yes, that would be stupid for someone to do, right?" She faked a sarcastic masculine voice, sounding like a cartoon character. "I lost my bong, man. Anybody seen it?"

They both laughed, the tension releasing. "Look, I'm sure your mom just wants to protect you. Maybe it would help if she could be around me, get to know me. Then she'll relax about it."

Amanda leaned back, propped on her elbows. "I don't know. Lately she's been acting weirder than usual. This crusade of hers against drugs, that's what's making her so suspicious. She's obsessed with it. And there's something even worse."

Her voice had dropped to a whisper, and her eyes held a serious look. Whatever it was had disturbed her. Big time. "What is it?"

"She's drinking. Alcohol, I mean. I found a flask in her purse. I've suspected it for a while, but now I'm certain. She might be an alcoholic."

Whatever he'd been expecting, this wasn't it. "Wow. That's ironic as hell. Well, there's not much you can do about it, especially if she won't admit it."

"I know." She lay back on the bed, her red hair in a halo around her head. She sighed, then changed the subject. "Hey, we never even talked about the Ouija Board."

He lay on the bed next to her, leaning on his elbow. "No, we haven't. What the hell was that, anyway? I never thought it would work like that."

"Me, too. But now that we know about Mark Fitzgill, what should we do?"

"We need to talk to him. Or I do. You don't need to get mixed up in this, Amanda."

She reached out, tapped a finger to his nose. "Too late. I'm too damn curious now. You can't get rid of me."

Something in the tone of her voice, and the glow in her warm copper eyes, caused his heart to pound. She licked her delicate pink lips then, a slow, furtive movement, like a cat stealing cream. She smelled of lilacs, and her skin was flushed from her chest to her face. They stared at one another for what seemed an eternity. He could hear her breath coming quicker, louder—or was that his own?

In an instant she rolled on top of him, pushing him back on the bed. His arms came around her and he could not pull her close enough. Their mouths were hungrily at war, tongues engaged in fierce play.

He had needed her, needed this, for so long. He could never escape the pain of what happened with Gina, but perhaps he could ease some of the pain Amanda was feeling. Perhaps he could love her enough to erase the agony of his own past, and lessen the guilt he felt by doing something good for someone else.

His hands roamed her body, feeling every curve. He wanted to absorb her into his skin, become one with her. Touching her was not enough. He couldn't find the usual words of protest, did not have the willpower to push her away this time. He knew she wanted to be his, and he wanted to be hers. Logic and reason had no place here, and for the first time, he knew it was meant to be.

She pulled away, her lips swollen and reddish-pink. "Please Zac, let me stay this time. Don't push me away."

He responded by flipping her over, onto her back. He laced his hands in hers. "I won't. I'll never send you away again."

And then he kissed her, pouring his overflowing feelings into every touch. It was as though a damn had burst, and he surprised himself with how deeply he felt it. But for now, he only wanted to make exquisite love to her, so no matter what happened later, she would never forget him, her first lover.

Amanda's heart was pounding loudly, blood rushing through every part of her. Her skin was on fire, and every place Zac touched her warmed. He was holding her wrists together above her head with one hand, as though she was going to struggle or try to get away. She no intention of doing so, but found the way he immobilized her added to the excitement.

He's making love to me. He's taken charge.

The idea thrilled her to the bone. For so long, she had been the pursuer, trying to break down his gentlemanly defenses. To have him not only give in but take control excited her more than any of her girlish fantasies ever had.

His other hand was unbuttoning her denim blouse in a slow tease while he kissed his way down her neck to her collar bone. She had worn her favorite black lace bra, and saw his startled reaction, followed by a knowing smile. "I see you've dressed for the occasion, Miss Bresky."

She blushed at that, and let out a sigh as his long, slender fingers slipped inside her bra. "Only for you," she whispered.

The bra had a clasp in the center of her breasts, which he undid with two fingers. She watched his face as he exposed her breasts, and saw only pleasure there. Closing his eyes, he leaned down to take one of her hardened nipples into his mouth.

Squirming and moaning, she threw her head back as he took his time exploring her breasts. She'd gone this far with boys before, but their efforts had been clumsy, more for their amusement than to please her. Before now, she'd no idea of the fine line between pleasure and torture a delicate touch could render.

"Oh, my God. Zac…."

His grip on her wrists relaxed. "Do you like this? Do you want me to stop?"

"Yes, I mean, no…don't stop. I love it."

She said the last part in a small voice, embarrassed to admit how much she was enjoying his attentions. But this was what she'd wanted for so long. There was no turning back now.

"Good. Tell me to stop if you change your mind. But if you don't stop me, I'm going to do everything I've wanted to do to you since the night we met. Just warning you."

His words made her toes curl. She wanted it, everything he wanted. But she pulled away, and stood up. "I've always wanted you, too. So do with me what you will."

Her blouse, bra, and skirt fell to the floor, followed by her panties. She stood naked, feeling bold and shy at the same time. He pulled her to him, and nuzzled her stomach. His beard tickled her, and her hands smoothed his wild, bushy mane. His cocoa-dark eyes looked up at her, then he smiled, opening a drawer in the dresser next to the bed. He pulled out a condom and lay it on the top of the dresser.

Oh my God, we're really doing this.

Seeing the condom had jarred her into reality. The moment she'd dreamed of for so long was about to happen. She watched as he slid his boxers to the floor, his cock—she blushed again, to think of it that way—standing at attention between his legs. She stared at it impolitely, unable to look away. He pulled her to him and lay her back on the bed again, the heat of his cock against her leg startling her.

They were kissing again, slow, passionate kisses that took her breath away. His hand strayed down her stomach, to her hip bone, then gently nudged her thighs apart. She opened them, and her obedience was rewarded. His fingers explored her outer lips with light, stroking motions. She felt a rush of heat and wetness, which intensified as his fingers found her nub. Rubbing in a circular pattern with his hand, he simultaneously nibbled on her breast. She felt the pleasure, almost a burn deep within her, starting to build. She'd pleasured herself before, but it was nothing like this. Having someone else doing delicious things to you while you lay there, helpless, was incredibly freeing.

She cried out as the pleasure peaked, and spams of joy rocked her insides. The thought that he had made her come, just by his touch, nearly made her cry. And he hadn't even been inside her yet.

But now she desperately wanted him to be there, inside her. As the waves of her orgasm subsided, she reached down to feel him. His length and width surprised her; she had stolen looks at the crotch of his jeans now and then, but had been unable to envision how it might look. Now it was smooth and warm and hard in her hand, and she let her fingers roam as he had done for her. "Please, Zac. Now. Make love to me."

He didn't say a word, but the look on his face told her he was more than ready. He moved away and slipped on the condom as she positioned herself more comfortably on the pillows. In a moment he settled over her, resting on his elbows. "If you get uncomfortable, tell me to stop."

She only nodded, and clung to him as he moved forward. She felt him nudging his way into her opening, and she had a moment of panic. Pressure turned into a full feeling as he slid inside, and she felt a moment of burning pain. She gasped involuntarily, and he rested for a moment. His eyes looked into hers, questioning, waiting for her to react. She realized how tense she was, so she willed herself to relax, and the pain subsided. She let out a breath and hugged his neck. "You're inside me."

"Yes I am. God, you're tight."

"I should hope so- ahh!"

He'd begun moving, almost pulling out, then forward again, in a rhythm which teased her insides with every stroke. Her hands on his back were slick, as was the place where their chests met. It was the sweat of their labor, and she enjoyed the feeling of being that close. He held her to him as he plunged into her, and slipped one hand under the small of her back, tilting her up. It was then she felt the tightening, the rush deep inside, and she cried out again.

Zac's groan in her ear told her he was close, and he stiffened, followed by a final thrust before collapsing on top of her.

She loved the feel of his weight on her, the sound of his breath in her ear. He lay still for a minute, then pulled away with a groan. Her body suddenly felt empty without him, her first lover. She hoped his earlier words were true, and not just said in a moment of passion. She couldn't bear it if he pulled away from her again, not just his body, but his heart.

14 Barriers

By late afternoon, Peggy's anxiety over the preparations for the rally had eased. Everyone in the M.A.I.D.s group had showed up to help, and their enthusiasm was contagious. For hours, they drew up posters, decided who would handle what, and organized their print material for handing out to the crowd. Peggy was certain the rally would be a success, if they could convince the community to embrace their cause with as much interest as these ladies had.

She couldn't help but feel a sense of pride, at having brought the group together. They not only applauded her ideas, but added a few of their own, the result being much more fruitful than she had anticipated. "Ladies, I must say I'm thrilled. We've accomplished quite a bit in the short time we've been working together. Now that we're done for the day, how about we celebrate? I've a bottle of bubbly that's been in the back of the fridge since New Year's."

The ladies murmured their agreement, all except Bridget, the teacher, who opted for lemon-lime soda instead. "It's still bubbly, isn't it?" she quipped. The ladies all toasted her, and each other, sipping their sparkling wine. The conversations went from the rally to personal matters as the group relaxed.

"For me, this was a way to give back to the community," Margo observed. Then her voice softened. "I had no idea it was going to become so personal, though."

The various conversations stopped, and all eyes were on Margo. Peggy held her breath, tempted to stop her friend from discussing the incident with her grandson, but Margo plowed ahead. "I just recently discovered some drug paraphernalia in my grandson's room." At the gasps around her, she nodded. "I was shocked, to say the least. But Peggy helped me to identify what it was, and I was able to keep Seth from getting into trouble. Although, he of course denied that it was his."

Exhaling slowly, Peggy joined in the comments of support for Margo. When the room quieted again, she noticed one of the ladies, Harriet, had her head in her hands.

"Harriet, are you okay?" She'd gone to stand in front of her, and knelt down. Harriet was always the quiet one, forever smiling. Now a muffled sob came from behind her hand.

The group gathered around, speaking in sympathetic tones. Someone offered a tissue, and she took it, sniffing. She raised her head, and looked at Peggy with reddened eyes. Eyes that held conviction. Her protective barrier of quiet observance had come down, and she was ready to talk. "For me, it's very personal. And I thought I'd be able to handle it, but now I'm not so sure."

Several of the ladies looked to Peggy for guidance, pain for their friend evident on their faces. When she looked back at Harriet, the woman had straightened up, and was wiping the tears from her eyes. Peggy spoke softly, hoping to soothe the poor woman. "You don't have to talk about it, dear. Unless you want to."

"No, maybe I should unburden myself. I've been sworn to secrecy for so long, but keeping it in has been killing me. Perhaps it's time to tell the truth."

Peggy re-filled Harriet's glass, and she drank a large sip, bolstering herself for her confession. Everyone watched, the only sound in the room the soft ticking of Peggy's grandfather clock in the corner.

"My niece died because of drugs. There, I've said it."

When no one spoke, she continued, relief evident in her shaky voice. "She didn't do it on purpose, though. She trusted her boyfriend, who supposedly didn't know it was laced with something really bad. The autopsy showed three different kinds of drugs in her system, and they never told me what exactly, but I know it was bad enough to mess her up. And it messed up my brother—her father—pretty bad, too, losing his little girl that way."

Peggy sat next to her on the sofa, and touched Harriet's shoulder in support. "How did it happen? An overdose?"

"Sort of. She and the boy were at Horse Tail reservoir, just after their graduation from high school, over a year ago. He gave her some dope to smoke, and whatever was in it made her go crazy. She jumped into the lake and drowned, after hitting the rocks near the shore. She didn't have a chance."

The woman broke down in tears again, and they let her sob. Wanda, the nurse, was sitting on the other side of her and rubbed her back, soothing her. Peggy handed her a box of tissues, and soon she raised her head to look around the room, as if to assess the trustworthiness of the group.

Harriet's tears subsided and she continued in a voice thick with regret. "You see, the boy's family was close friends with my brother and his wife, and they asked that the incident be kept quiet. But a year's gone by, and that boy was never charged, being under age at the time. He's eighteen, almost nineteen now. Old enough to take responsibility for what he did, I think. Even if he all he does is apologize to my brother's family, it would help in their grief."

The room suddenly erupted as the women all talked at once, offering words of encouragement for Harriet and their opinions on the situation. Peggy took it all in, realizing the effect the sad tale had on the group. She knew she'd be devastated if something like that ever happened to Mandy, or one of the boys. It struck her that this situation had the potential to boldly illustrate what could happen when children played with drugs. She spoke loud enough to be heard over the din of voices.

"Ladies, this is the very thing Walter Jackson, our Sheriff, has been warning people about. It's bad enough when kids experiment with this stuff, but they often get more than they bargained for, don't they?"

Agreement from the group was quick and enthusiastic. If the townspeople knew someone had actually died as a result of the bad drugs being passed around, they would be able to raise so much more money. Donations would soar, and their group would be well known. And it just might prevent such horrors from happening to someone else.

A plan formed in her mind, and to celebrate, she emptied the last of the sparkling wine into her glass, and raised it for a toast. "To Harriet. I hope you find peace in your heart. Such a tragedy should never have happened, but know this—we are going to do everything we can to safeguard the citizens, and especially the children of Powder County, from the dangers of illegal drugs."

The other women raised their glasses, though a few were empty. To a chorus of "Hear, hear", Peggy drained her glass, wishing for a fleeting moment it was something stronger.

~*~

By four o'clock, they were famished. They had explored each other thoroughly, and Zac was amazed how quickly Amanda's initial shyness had turned into unbridled lust. His straight-laced good girl definitely had a wild, wanton side to her. And he loved it.

"I'll treat you to a burger at Trinket's Diner before you go home. We can use the phone book they keep by the payphone to see if we can find Mark Fitzgill, too."

She agreed, and they were dressed and out the door minutes later. He should have been exhausted, but felt pleasantly energized. He had no regrets about bedding her, and wished he'd done it sooner. There may still be complications to come—like her parents, for example—but he felt so great at the moment, he didn't care. Whatever went wrong in the future was worth it. He couldn't wait to take her again, and longed to spend the night in her arms. But knew that would only make things more difficult for her at home, so he didn't even suggest it.

One step at a time, buddy.

Once they had fortified themselves with greasy burgers and crisp, equally greasy fries, Amanda brought the battered phone book to their table. She sipped on her root beer as she flipped through the pages, finally stopping, murmuring,

"F....Farmer...Felton...Fitz...here it is. Benton Fitzgill. It's the only Fitzgill in here."

Zac pulled a pen from his pocket, hand poised to write on a napkin. "Must be his father. What's the address and number?"

"It's 4769 Town Cliff Road. That's out in that fancy new subdivision. They must have money." She then recited the phone number, which he scribbled on the napkin.

"I'll take a drive out there, see if I can talk to him. I probably won't get through if I try to call. They'd think I'm a nut."

"Yeah, they're still going to think that, anyway. I should come with you, so it doesn't seem creepy."

A half hour later, they'd found the house. The subdivision was filled with large, two-story homes, but the streets were quiet. He got the sense it was a stay-to-yourself kind of neighborhood, not like the one he grew up in. "This ain't New Jersey, all right. Everybody'd be on their stoops at this time of evening, shooting the breeze."

Amanda smiled at his observation as she emerged from the car. They walked up to the house, and he noted there was no car in the driveway, but the garage door was open, showing a small Honda motorcycle at the back of the garage. He wondered if it belonged to the guy they were hoping to meet. It might give him something to talk about, to break the ice.

He hadn't thought of what to say until now, and he had a moment of panic as Amanda rang the doorbell. Seconds later a woman answered, blonde hair teased high on her head, dressed as though she were going out for the evening, to a dinner party or fancy event. He waved awkwardly, thinking she probably wouldn't shake his hand. "Uh, hi, Ma'am. We're looking for Mark Fitzgill."

Her green eyes, lined heavily in dark eyeliner, and rimmed with a fringe of fake eyelashes, looked them over as though they were something that crawled from the trash can. He understood the woman's judgement of him, but Amanda looked proper, and although she still had the glow of a thoroughly-loved woman, he was certain no one else could tell but him.

"Who are you?" she blurted out. Her eyes traveled over each of them, and her hand was on the door, ready to close it.

Amanda jumped in. "We're old friends from school. We were just in the neighborhood and wanted to say hi. Is he home?"

The woman's eyes narrowed, and she looked over her shoulder. When she faced them again, she shook her head, the stiffly lacquered brown hair not moving. "He's not feeling well right now. I'll let him know you stopped by, um…?"

The incline of her head indicated her question, and they both spoke at once, telling her their names. Amanda handed the woman a napkin, on which she had scrawled her home phone number. "Tell him to call me, please, so we can catch up."

The woman nodded and closed the door.

"Well that went well," Amanda grumbled as they reached the VW Beetle. "I'll let you know if he ever calls."

"Good idea, giving him your number. He might call if he hears a strange but beautiful redhead was looking for him."

"I doubt that's how his mom will describe me, but thanks."

Once in the car, he pulled her close. "That's how I'll always describe you."

She kissed him, saying, "And I'd describe you as pretty strange, too, Fuzzy."

He laughed at that, and put the car in gear, changing the subject. "You know, I just want to tell this guy what I know, and be done with it. I don't really care what he did, or who was at fault. Maybe then the ghost of Paige Rothmeyer will leave me alone."

"We can only hope. If not, we'll just have to buy an Ouija board."

~*~

Amanda steeled herself for her mother's wrath when she walked in the door at seven that evening. The anger she felt about what she overheard on the phone that morning lingered, but she didn't have the desire for confrontation just yet. Presently her thoughts were focused on replaying the delicious afternoon she'd had in Zac's bed, and she wanted the feeling to last as long as possible.

To her surprise, everyone ignored her. Her father kissed her cheek as he and the boys passed on their way to shoot hoops in the driveway. Peggy was at the dining room table, engrossed in writing her speech for the next day's rally. The only question she asked Amanda was if she planned to be at the rally to show her support.

"Of course, Mom. I'll be there."

She climbed the stairs to her room, grateful for the chance to be alone. There was a pleasant soreness between her legs, which made her smile when she thought of how she'd earned it. She decided a hot bath was in order.

Later, soaking in a tub of fragrant bubbles, she couldn't help but move her hands over her body, recalling how he'd touched her in ways she'd never been touched before. Her breath caught and her heart accelerated, the mental image of his naked body enough to send her nearly to the edge. She wanted more, needed more. She craved his touch like one of those addictive drugs her mother was always freaking out about.

She'd done it. Finally succeeded in her mission to get Zac to make love to her. *So now what?*

Despite the warm water, a chill raised bumps on her arms. He had protested and avoided her for a reason, though she never understood what that was. Sure, he was being gentlemanly, which made her want him all the more, but was that the only reason? They were good friends, but she really knew so little about him.

He never talked much about his past, or his life in New Jersey, aside from mentioning food he missed or various customs that differed from Colorado. She knew he'd had a rough time after he first arrived in the state, and that whatever happened had caused him to get into drugs and alcohol in a bad way. He overcame it, though—got clean and sober, and had supposedly been that way for a few years now.

She had taken him into her body, and as a result, he was now in her heart more than ever. Would he let her inside his heart? Or was it just casual sex, as he'd warned her all along?

"Who are you, Zac Daley?" she whispered, her hand patting at the bubbles on the water's surface. "And are you going to break my heart?"

15 Messengers

"Write a letter. Tell him."

Zac was pulled from a deep sleep with the sensation of being touched. He reached for Amanda, but it was an empty pillow at his side, not the warm, soft feminine form his hands longed to touch. He thought he saw her from the corner of his eye, catching a movement in the darkness. Fear gripped him as he came fully awake, aware he was alone, but also peering at the shadowy figure just at the foot of his bed.

It was there, but not really there, in the way fog mists over the ground, but you can still see through it. Roughly the size of a human, the shadow took shape for a moment, and he recognized it as the same girl he saw at the lake, standing by the bush.

She faded, then reappeared, and again he heard the words, "Tell him. Write a letter."

He hadn't really heard the words with his ears so much as with his thoughts, his mind. Which was unbelievably freaky. His throat was tight with fear, but he had to answer her. "Okay, I'll do it. Tell him what, Paige?"

Maybe addressing the ghost directly would make her seem less scary. He didn't get the sense she meant him any harm, yet it was still creeping him out. Her face was obscured, and he saw no movement of her lips. But the words came to his mind, as though she'd shouted.

"Not his fault. Accident. Save him."

Then she faded into the darkness. He flipped on the lamp at his bedside to find an empty room, and no trace of any disturbance. He moved quickly to the table, searching for a pen and paper to write down what happened.

Why did Mark Fitzgill need to be saved? From what? As far as he could tell, the kid hadn't been charged with anything, and was laying low at his parent's house. Probably playing his Atari or watching Gilligan's Island reruns.

But it really didn't matter what the kid was doing with his time. He'd write the damn letter, if it would make these midnight visits stop. He had no idea how he'd ended up being a cosmic messenger for a disembodied spirit, anyhow.

As he sat down to write the letter, he looked across the table, and there was the culprit. The vintage camera Amanda had given him. Somehow it had attracted the Drowning Girl's spirit, and here he was writing a letter in the middle of the night, because a ghost asked him to. He wasn't one to philosophize, but he understood that sometimes things that seem crazy or horrible have a higher purpose in the end.

Even horrible things like crashing your car, and losing the love of your life?

He flinched at the memory, his gut twisting with grief. Four years had not erased the images of that night from his mind, or the longing for lost love from his heart. Loss and grieving could make a person do things they might not normally do. Maybe that was why Paige was worried—she knew that Mark was still grieving and she wanted to ease his pain.

He shook his head to clear it, and picked up a pen to write the letter. Maybe someday, this would all make sense. For now, he'd play along until the meaning became clear.

~*~

The crowds were starting to arrive, many of them dressed in patriotic red, white and blue clothing. Peggy and the other M.A.I.D.s ladies were dressed similarly, and wearing large buttons with their group name and logo. The sun was blazing, though it was only ten a.m., and Peggy smiled at Victor as he brought the cooler full of drinks from the car to place it under the table at her feet.

"I left the boys with Mrs. Gumbolt. She'll watch them while they hang out with her son, she said."

"Thanks, honey," Peggy said, relieved. Two less things to worry about. The boys had done their part to help her, even if they had been pressed into service. Let them enjoy the day with their friend. Her wayward daughter, on the other hand…

"Vic, have you seen Amanda? I thought she'd be here by now."

He shook his head, and went off to carry the rest of her posters from the car. Everything was almost ready—the ladies were at their stations passing out fliers, and she'd rehearsed her speech dozens of times. The Mayor was due to arrive any moment to proclaim the rally underway, and then it would be her turn to shine.

She'd snuck into the nearby restroom earlier to take a sip of courage from her flask. Then she popped a breath mint to cover it up, although who could blame her for attempting to calm her nerves? About to face her largest crowd ever, she shook with a mixture of anticipation and fear. It was no one else's business how she conducted herself in private, anyway.

She noticed Mayor Keswick approaching, his wife and son in tow. "Good morning, Mayor, Mrs. Keswick. Happy Independence Day."

They made small talk for a few minutes, and the Mayor seemed impressed with the materials she and the other ladies were passing out. As the Mayor climbed the steps to the platform, his wife whispered in Peggy's ear. "I understand there are some investors in town who are considering building a rehabilitation center out at the old Aggie Farm location. Perhaps your group might be interested in helping to seek out donations."

Peggy's heart rate jumped. To be involved in such a project would be a dream come true. Her mind immediately began spinning with prospects. "Are any of them here, now?"

Mrs. Keswick looked around at the crowd. "Could be, some of them are locals, though most are from Denver, I'm told."

"I would definitely be interested. Please have them contact me."

Mrs. Keswick smiled and shook her hand. Then the sound of her name over the loudspeakers sent a fresh jolt of apprehension through her.

"…and now, to kick off our 4th of July rally, here is Peggy Bresky with an important announcement."

The Mayor's introduction shunted her conversation with his wife, and she went to take her place at the podium. As she looked out and greeted the crowd, she noticed Amanda had arrived, and was standing by the table with her father, watching.

After a short introduction and explanation of the purpose of forming the M.A.I.D.s, she launched into the meat of her speech.

"But fighting the influx of illegal drugs in our county is more than just a noble cause. For most of the folks who have attended the meetings, but especially for the other M.A.I.D.s ladies, and yes, even myself, the cause is a personal one. Many of us have faced the heartbreak of having a friend or loved one in trouble, due to drug abuse. It is not only disruptive to a family to face addiction, with the resulting financial and/or legal troubles. It is sometimes much worse. It can all be quite devastating. Some families, and some individuals, unfortunately never recover."

The crowd had gone somber, so she knew her words were making an impact. "Imagine how you all would feel, if a family member wasn't here with you today, because they were injured, or even killed, due to taking drugs? Yes, folks, it happens, and it happened here in Powder County, just last year."

She saw wide eyes, and open mouths, so she dropped the bomb. "A young girl, barely out of high school, smoked dope with her boyfriend out at Horse Tail reservoir, just as many kids have likely done before. But this time," she paused for effect," the marijuana had been tampered with. Other chemicals were added and it made her go crazy. Crazy enough to jump off the cliff into the lake, where she hit the rocks and then drowned."

The gasps and expressions of shock told her she had hit her mark. Now to draw them in.

"What is one child's, perhaps your own child's, life worth? Any donation you can give today will go a long way for our organization. We plan to work tirelessly to make Powder County safe for families again. Stop by our table, where you can sign a petition to keep out businesses that cater to the illegal drug trade. Or you can make a donation, which will go toward funding our efforts to bring drug education seminars to our schools. We can also refer families in need of assistance in coping with drug problems, to programs such as counseling, or even rehabilitation."

Time to lighten it up, leave them feeling good. "We have flags, buttons, and other goodies, too. So please stop by and say hello. And watch for us around town, the M.A.I.D.s have just begun their mission to clean up Powder County. Happy Fourth of July, everyone!"

Her heart was pounding so hard, it rang in her ears. The crowd cheered and clapped until she stepped down from the platform. Several people rushed toward their table, and she beamed as the ladies jumped to attention to help. It was then she noticed Harriet glowering at her, but Victor swept her up in a hug before she could investigate.

~*~

It was mid-morning when Zac made it to Mark Fitzgill's neighborhood, with his letter in hand. He'd parked a few houses away, hoping no one would see him approach and they would actually answer the door. He had a feeling the boy's mother would not be happy to see him again, and alone this time. He wished there was another way to get to Mark without running a gauntlet. It seemed silly to mail it, and the holiday would have delayed the mail anyway.

As it was, he knocked on the door several times, but no one answered. He was unsure whether to leave it in the mailbox at the door, or come back another day. But the image of his midnight visitor made his skin turn to bumps, so he stood there on the sidewalk, trying to decide what to do.

"Hey Mister, do you have a dime?"

He looked down to see a tow-headed boy of about nine pushing a bicycle down the sidewalk toward him. Decked out with glittery red paint, the bike had a banana seat and spider handlebars, complete with tassels hanging off the ends. He figured the kid must be the envy of his friends with that thing.

"Maybe. Why?"

Curiosity and amusement at the child's bold question made him answer. He was dressed too well and the bicycle too shiny for him to be poor. Especially in this neighborhood.

"Cause my tire needs air, and that's what it costs at the gas station. Mark usually gives me some, he has an air pump. But he's not home today."

Zac dug in his pocket, coming up with the dime. He handed it to the boy, asking, "You know Mark Fitzgill?"

"Yeah, I live next door. He's probably at the doctor's."

"On the Fourth of July? That's odd."

The boy shrugged. "He's always at the doctor's lately. Or hiding in his room. Sometimes he works on his motorcycle, though. He lets me watch."

"That's cool. So, what's your name?"

"Timmy Lockmore."

"Well, Timmy, how would you like to make a whole dollar?"

The boy looked up at him, suddenly interested. "What do I have to do?"

Zac's fingers pulled a dollar bill from his pocket, and he held it where the boy could get a good look at it. "All you have to do is see that Mark gets this letter as soon as possible." He held the envelope up next to the dollar. "Can you do that?"

"Sure. I'll just keep an eye out for when he gets home."

"Can you try to slip it to him when his mom's not looking? It's kind of a private message, a secret."

The kid's blue eyes bugged out, then narrowed. "Make it two dollars, then. And I promise I won't open it."

The last bit made him pause, but he didn't have much choice. Is he related to Wes Porter, I wonder? He couldn't keep coming back here, waiting for Mark to show his face.

"Okay. But keep it safe until you can give it to Mark." He handed the envelope to Timmy, who was pushing his bike back to his own house. "And I'll be back here soon to make sure he got, it, too," he called as Timmy disappeared up his own driveway.

16 Confrontations

Amanda waited impatiently as her mother shook hands and kissed babies, behaving more like a politician than a mother stumping for a good cause. As she paced, the summer heat bore down on her without any hint of a breeze, and her stomach grumbled. She'd overslept, the events of yesterday and her long soak in the tub putting her into a near coma of deep sleep. It was the first peaceful night she'd had in a long while, but it put her behind schedule and she hadn't had time to eat. If she had missed her mother's speech she would never hear the end of it.

Now she wished she hadn't heard it, stunned as she was to hear Peggy mention Paige's death. How the hell did she know about that? Had Walter told her?

But that wasn't what worked on her right now. The mention of Paige's drowning had thrown her over the edge, but what first pissed her off was the holier-than-thou, my-heart-bleeds rest of her mother's speech. Like Peggy Bresky was some sort of saint, fit to judge others' actions. The hypocrisy of what she just heard and what she knew to be true about her mother, sparked her anger to firecracker level.

"Mom." She tugged at her mother's sleeve, which was ignored. Another woman had pulled her aside and they were speaking in hushed tones, and the other woman seemed angry with Peggy, too. Amanda stepped back, listening.

"I told you that in confidence. I never dreamed you'd broadcast it to the whole county."

Peggy was attempting to diffuse the woman's ire. She wasn't succeeding. "Now, no names were mentioned. It really touched people's hearts, Harriet. That's a good thing. Look how many-"

The woman pulled off her M.A.I.D. button, and threw it on the table. "I don't give a damn. That was private information, and you abused my trust. I'm done with this. I'm done with *you.*"

People started gawking, and Peggy smiled, pretending all was well. Harriet stomped off, and the other ladies looked around, questioning.

"Mom."

Peggy exhaled, and finally looked at her daughter. "What, Mandy? Can't you see I am overwhelmed at the moment?"

A good daughter would have backed off. A good daughter would have been at her side helping with her cause.

But a good mother never would have done the things she'd done. Amanda didn't understand how things had gone so wrong, she only knew she couldn't take it anymore.

She pulled on Peggy's arm, and dragged her behind the platform. Loud music started as a group of kids from the local high school's marching band started their patriotic music set. Amanda had to yell to be heard, but she would be heard this time.

"Mom, I know you think you're doing the right thing. But it kills me to see you get up there and act like you know everything. You're passing judgment on people without knowing anything about them. Like you did with Zac. Not to mention, you're hiding your own bad behavior behind a good cause."

An open-mouthed stare was all the response she got. Then Peggy's normally pinkish cheeks turned red as apples.

"Who do you think you are, young lady? All I've ever done is cater to you, and give you everything you wanted and needed. How ungrateful can you—"

She grabbed her mother's wrist, and her attention. "Mom, this is not about me, not about all that. What about your drinking? I found the flask in your purse."

Peggy pulled her wrist away as if it burned. "Snooping through my things? Oh Lord. If we weren't in public, I'd..."

"What, Mom? Would you hit me? I just think it's time you admitted you aren't a saint. You're just as much a sinner as those you condemn."

Amanda wasn't expecting the hand that did smack her, right across her cheek. It stung, but she knew she'd done it. That untouched place in Peggy's soul, where she hid her dark secrets, was now exposed.

Peggy's response was laced with venom. "I'll deal with you later."

She watched her mother return to the crowd, head held high, fake smile plastered on her face. Amanda rubbed her cheek, the sting fading to a warmth. "Yes, Mom. I'm sure you will."

~*~

At one a.m., Zac finished up the last of the cleanup at the bar. They'd closed early, at midnight, since they weren't as busy as the owner thought they were going to be. A few small bands of revelers had straggled in after the fireworks show at the park was through, but they hadn't stayed long.

He was grateful for the break, exhausted as he was from his lack of sleep the night before. He'd been up most of the night drafting the letter to Mark, and then was unable to sleep, even with the light on. He still wasn't used to communing with a ghost, even though he knew she meant him no harm. He had no idea if Tommy Lockmore had delivered the letter as promised, but he sincerely hoped so. He'd tried to convey a sense of concern and urgency in his letter, and Mark Fitzgill would take from it what he would. The matter was out of his hands now. But if the boy wanted to talk, he could call, as both Zac's phone number and the number for the bar were in the letter.

Exiting through the back, he turned out the lights and locked the door. Pale moonlight lit the parking area, but he was so used to it, he could probably find his car if it was pitch black. As he stuck his key in the door, a noise to his left startled him. Thinking it was the stray cat he'd seen hanging around, he turned to find himself facing not a feral cat but two large men.

"What do you—"

The words were barely out of his mouth when the taller one punched him in the stomach, causing him to choke on his words. The impact was almost as bad as the crash, and images of that night exploded in his mind. He bent over, trying to breathe, and rough hands grabbed his collar and slammed him against his car.

The taller man held him there, immobilized. His captor's face was twisted in a menacing sneer, and the stench of beer and cigarettes nearly made Zac gag. Through blurred eyes, he saw the man's head was covered in salt and pepper hair, shaved into a buzz cut. The hands that still gripped his collar were meaty, with oil-stained, fat fingers. *Must be some kind of laborer, or a mechanic.*

The shorter man drew closer, waving a cigarette. "We're not here to rob ya, Granola Boy. Just to warn you."

Then he held the cigarette out, stopping a mere inch away from Zac's bushy hair. His fingers were also stained, and grimy around the nails. He smelled of gasoline, and Zac wondered what the hell they wanted from him. "Warn me of what? I don't know what the hell you're talking about."

Instead of answering, the shorter man with the cigarette still taunted him, now waving the glowing tip just inches from Zac's beard. He was wearing a white tank top, and a straw cowboy hat. The two didn't look like they belonged together at all, but here they were. Cowboy Hat then took a drag, blowing the smoke in Zac's face, leering but saying nothing more.

It was the taller man, Buzz Cut, who spoke. "We're here to tell you to stay away from Mark. No visits. No letters. No calls. No nothin'. Ya got that, Granola Boy?"

He backed away, along with Cowboy Hat, who sneered, "If ya don't get it, we'll have to get tough next time. Dig?"

With that, they faded into the night. He stood against his car until his breath came normally again. *What the hell?* Why on earth would Mark have two thugs come after him? He didn't see how he could possibly pose a threat to the boy. He realized now it was a mistake to mention where he worked in the letter, but he thought maybe it would seem friendlier to give some personal details. He knew he already sounded like a kook, quoting a girl who had passed on, but there was no other way to say it.

What just happened did not make any sense, and he wanted nothing more to do with the whole thing. It wasn't worth it. Sitting in his car, he put the engine in gear and drove home, watching over his shoulder. No one followed. He was safe, for the moment.

~*~

Amanda whispered to Zac, leaning over the library check-in counter to get a good look at him. He didn't seem to be hurt, and she thanked God. "What do you mean, they roughed you up? Who were they?"

"They punched me good in the stomach, but I'm okay. I was about to beat the crap out of them, when they took off."

"Oh." She wasn't sure about that, although she had no doubt Zac could take care of himself, if he had to. She repressed the feeling of panic that was welling up and tried to remain calm. "Well, I guess it means he got the letter and now we can back off. It's not worth you getting hurt."

He leaned over, his voice low. "My guess is, his parents intercepted the letter, and sent someone to discourage me. I can't imagine Mark himself sending out thugs to do his dirty work. The letter was not that inflammatory."

"What exactly did you say?"

"I said something like, 'This may sound crazy, but I have a message from Paige. Her ghost has visited me numerous times, and she insists that I tell you that what happened to her was not your fault. She wants you to be safe and happy, and she does not blame you.' And then I told him where I worked, the phone number there, and if he wanted to talk more, to call me."

Amanda let out a breath. "Well…I guess that was safer than telling him where you lived, or giving him your home number. But it does sound crazy, though I can't think of any better way to say it."

"I wish the damn ghost would have just visited him, and told him herself."

"Maybe she has, but he wasn't ready to listen." She couldn't believe she was talking about this, but so many strange things had happened lately, and she had a feeling it wasn't over.

"Well, I'm done being her messenger. Now it's time for me to get my ass in gear, and get on with my life."

"Which means what? Are you going to leave?" She couldn't keep the panic from her voice this time, and he took her hand in his.

"I don't know. If I don't find a job here in town soon, I'll have no choice but to move on. I gotta pay for my degree somehow."

What he said made sense. There wasn't much opportunity in Fort Winston for a journalism major, or a photographer. Unless….

"Hey, have you checked with the Office of Tourism and Development? It's a new part of the city government. My dad works for the county, and he heard about it. They might need someone with your skills, don't you think?"

"It's worth a try. Think they'll be open today?"

She gave him the address of the county office, where he could get more information on where to apply. The ice that encased her heart at the thought of him leaving, thawed just a little. As he turned to leave, she added, "Oh. And Fuzzy, comb your hair, maybe?"

He rolled his eyes and blew her a kiss, disappearing out the door.

When her shift was through, she headed straight to Mark's neighborhood. She parked in front of the house next door, and waited. It wasn't long before she spotted him, a little blond boy who looked just as Zac had described, fancy bicycle and all. A boy who had some explaining to do.

Before he could hop on his bike, she called from her car. She got out, and introduced herself. "Hi, my name's Amanda. My friend gave you a letter to give to Mark?"

The boy looked wary, answering, "So?"

"Well, did you give it to him?"

"Yeah. Then his dad came in the garage while he was reading it. Mark threw it in the trash and went inside. His dad told me to go home."

"Oh. Did Mark seem upset?"

"I don't know. Can I go now?"

"Sure."

She eyed Mark's house, tempted to try to speak with him, but she didn't want them coming after Zac again. *So it probably was Mark's dad who sent the thugs...*

"Hey, Timmy." When the boy stopped, looking at her over his shoulder, she asked, "What does Mark's dad do? Do you know where he works? I need to talk to him."

"He owns the gas station, at the corner. Everybody knows that."

Timmy took off, jumping his bicycle off the curb and whizzing down the street. There was a gas station near the entrance to the subdivision, she'd take a look on her way out. Zac would be upset if he knew she was here, but she had to know what was really going on. She didn't want him to leave town because of all this.

She didn't want him to leave town for any reason, ever, but that was another day's battle.

17 Making Amends

The clerk at the gas station had been friendly and chatty, providing the information Amanda needed. A little flirting didn't hurt, and the young man seemed happy to brag about where he worked as he filled her gas tank and cleaned her windshield. The Fitzgill family owned not only this station, but several others, stretching from Ft. Winston to Denver. Each station had a garage attached, where repairs and oil changes were done. Three rough-looking mechanics also gave her the eye as she went inside to pay for the gas and grab a cold drink.

He's probably just protecting his son. But they still had no right to punch Zac....

Her thoughts wandered as she drove home. Zac said he was done, so she should be, too. But something nagged at her, adding to her apprehension as she neared her house. Her mother had been giving her the cold shoulder since their confrontation yesterday, and that bothered her, too. She felt a twinge of guilt over her part in it, but it would be worth it if her mother would ease up on the drinking.

When she got home, Peggy was in a lawn chair in the backyard, reading a magazine. The boys were playing on the swing set, and the aroma of something on the stove wafted through the screen door, making her suddenly hungry.

"Hi, Mom. I'm sorry about yesterday."

Peggy didn't look up, eyes glued to the glossy pages. "Well, you should be. As it was, the day got better. We surpassed our goal for donations. Not that you care."

She sat on the back steps, a few feet away. "I do care, Mom. That's why I did it. I don't want to see you become an alcoholic."

That got her a look, and an eye roll. "I'm not. I just have a sip every now and then. It's no big deal. Nothing for you, or anyone else, to worry about."

"I hope so, I really do. By the way, who was that lady and why was she so mad at you?" She knew it had something to do with Paige's death, and her curiosity had been niggling at her since she witnessed the woman dressing her mother down.

"Oh, that was just Harriet. She's an emotional wreck because her niece died last year, due to drug abuse. I thought it would be okay to use her situation as an example, but she thought otherwise."

"Oh. She looked familiar. Isn't she the one who works downtown, at that flower shop?"

Peggy's face puzzled a moment, then she nodded. "You might be right, come to think of it. She brought a vase of red, white and blue carnations for our table at the rally."

"Oh. Well, I'm going upstairs to change. Need help with dinner?"

Peggy declined, and Amanda retreated to her room. Another truce with her mom. *Wonder how long this one will last?*

~*~

After applying for work at the Office of Tourism and Development, Zac spent the day cleaning his room, throwing out junk, and boxing up what was left. Jittery and restless, he paced back and forth, and only after hours of work did he realize what he was really trying to do. It was his heart, his mind, and his life that needed cleaning up, not his living quarters.

He missed her. After years of denial, trying to forget, he had to admit it or the longing and guilt would never cease. He'd come across an envelope full of photos while he cleaned, and now he sat there with moments of life he would never get back strewn across the table in front of him.

Gina and him at the zoo. Together at high school graduation. Christmas at her folk's house, next door to where he'd
lived all his life. They'd been friends since she moved in,
when they were both just nine years old. He'd teased her then,
sometimes until she cried, but he'd always loved her. He had
never imagined life with anyone else. It was a given they
would someday marry. They knew it, their families and their
friends knew it. They'd sing to him, *"Zac and Gina, sitting in
a tree...k-i-s-s-i-n-g!"*

But he'd just laugh, because there was no one else he
wanted to kiss, wanted to be with, or wanted to marry.

Until now. Until Amanda.

He pushed the thought away. *Yeah, her parents would love
that, a hairy hippie for a son-in-law.*

He had no job, no plans, and no business being with someone like her. Amanda was untouchable, a good girl who
should be spending her time with someone she might marry.
He couldn't promise her that, not now, maybe never. It was
wrong to tell her he'd never push her away again, but he'd
been intoxicated from making love to her. She'd never believe it, but he was certain deep down, she would be better off
without him.

He'd never be able to give himself fully to Amanda, or
anyone, until he made peace with his past. It was time to go
back to New Jersey and set things right. He hadn't been back
since the funeral. Not for the holidays, not for the summer.
His parents and friends had finally stopped trying to get him
to come home last year. They had all given up, and the occasional letter or phone call from them had become less frequent
as well.

When he came back to Colorado after burying Gina, he
had tried to go on alone. But the pain was so great, he'd underestimated the aftermath. To cope, he hid inside himself,
numbed with drugs and alcohol until a friend, his only real
friend in Colorado, intervened.

It was Sarah McKenn who set him straight. She was the
only one who told him what an ass he was being, and that

she'd no longer hang out with him and watch him kill himself with excess. Her words had pierced his pride like an arrow, and he took a hard look at himself, and made some changes. It wasn't easy, but he got himself clean and never looked back.

Placing the photos back in their envelope, he made a decision. He knew he had to face the darkness in his heart, one final time. He'd go home, and beg for forgiveness from Gina's family, and his own. He could stay in Colorado, he could travel the world, but that darkness would always be there. Perhaps if they could forgive him, someday he'd be able to forgive himself, as well.

~*~

Amanda had the day off, so she headed downtown around lunchtime to see if Harriet would speak with her. No one knew what she was doing, and if she found out nothing about what happened to Paige and Mark, it couldn't hurt. But she had a hunch, so she walked into the shop to find Harriet at the counter, arranging roses in a vase.

"Welcome. May I help you, young lady?"

"Hi. Harriet, is it? I'm Amanda, Peggy's daughter."

The friendly face turned sour at the mention of her mother's name, but Amanda continued. "I just wanted to apologize for my mother's behavior at the rally. She really meant well, but she should have discussed it with you first."

Harriet's frown softened, and she took the vase to a nearby table. She cut a length of white ribbon, and tied it about the vase. "Hmmph. Well, yes, she should have. Why doesn't she come here and tell this me herself?"

The woman fixed her with an indignant look. She really should have rehearsed this conversation, but she didn't know what to expect. "My mom doesn't know I'm here, but I'm sure she'll come see you soon. She can be a bit stubborn at times, but she means well. And I just hate to see two friends, especially ones joined in a good cause, at such odds with one another." When Harriet's face softened, she added, "I hope I'm not being too forward."

Amanda tried her best to seem humble, and it must have worked. Harriet handed her a pink carnation, and a then blue one. "Blue is the color of friendship. Tell your mother I'll try to make the next meeting."

Amanda sniffed the carnation, enjoying the spicy scent. "Thank you. I'll tell her. And, I was wondering, she said it was your niece who died up at the lake?"

Harriet's hands stilled, her face dropped. "Yes. My brother's girl. We really miss her."

"I'm sure you do. I'm so sorry for your loss."

Walking to a refrigerated cabinet, Harriet placed the vase inside. She turned back to Amanda, asking, "Did you know her?"

"No, but I think I remember the boy she was with. Mark, is it?"

"Yes, Mark Fitzgill. So sad. He survived, but he's been a mess since then. In and out of therapy," she lowered her voice to a whisper, though no one else was in the shop. "In fact, he's in the hospital right now. Tried to kill himself last night. Thank God, he didn't succeed. We don't need another tragedy."

Heat flared through her, jangling her nerves. *Suicide.* This was serious. Had Zac's letter pushed an emotionally fragile boy over the edge?

"Oh, my. I hope he'll be okay. He's at Powder County hospital?"

"Yes. My brother only said he had stabilized, but they are keeping him for a day or so. They had to pump out his stomach, but otherwise he's fine."

"Well, I hope he recovers. I have to be going now, and thanks for the flowers."

She left the flower shop and made a beeline to Zac's place. When he let her in, she noticed his room was clean, with boxes stacked neatly in a corner.

"What's wrong, Zac? Your place is spotless. Are you not feeling well?"

"Ha. Just cleaning up this shithole, for a change. What's up?"

She sensed there was more to it, but let it slide. "Mark Fitzgill is in the hospital. He tried to commit suicide last night."

He sat down, his face pale. "Oh, wow. I wonder if the letter... I hope-"

She cut him off, realizing he had to know the truth. "Yes, he did get the letter. I spoke with Timmy." At his dejected look, she added, "But that can't be the only reason. I found out he's been in therapy for months, he's been strung out since Paige died. So this incident can't be your fault."

He just looked at her with a pained expression, so she went to hug him, resting her head on his. He held onto her, and she moved to sit on his lap. He sat for a long moment holding her, silent. Then he spoke, his voice edged in frustration. "I know it's not directly my fault, but it probably didn't help. But what could I do? Paige wouldn't leave me alone."

She hugged him tight. It felt so good to have an easy intimacy with him, to be out of the friend zone. She no longer had to stay at arm's length. She was tempted to start seducing him, but the plan she'd crafted on the way over took priority for the moment.

"Well, Fuzzy, I have an idea, which might make you feel better." She moved from his lap to sit next to him, continuing her thoughts. "I think we should try to talk to Mark, to be sure he understands. He may have thought you were just some jerk trying to prank him."

"How can I get near him now? His father knows about me, and those thugs were pretty convincing."

She stood, looking at her watch. "Don't worry. I have a plan."

18 Flashbacks

Powder County Hospital was the last place he wanted to visit. It was where he'd been taken to that night of the crash, where they told him Gina was gone forever. He'd swore he'd never come back here voluntarily, yet here he was, following Amanda into the elevator.

He kept his breathing steady, fighting down a sense of panic. The place still smelled the same, an odd mixture of antiseptic and illness. Or was that his imagination? The artificial lights overhead made him blink, images of that night long ago starting surface in his mind. They had taken Gina in a different ambulance than him, and it was several agonizing hours before he could get anyone to tell him how she was. When they finally did, he wished they hadn't told him, so he could still imagine she might have survived. Those few hours were torture, but at least he still had a thread of hope.

The ding of the elevator door jarred him back to the task at hand, and he watched as Amanda stuck her head out to check the hallway. "It's clear," she whispered. They walked to a small seating area, which was empty and quiet except for the blare of a television. She instructed him to stay there, and to duck into the restroom if any one came by.

He watched her walk down the hall, peeking into the various rooms as she went. An orderly came around the corner pushing a cart, startling him, but walked by without a glance. Pacing between the two rows of chairs, he was unable to decide whether to leave the hospital or stay and see Amanda's plan through. Before he could obsess any further, she came back around the corner.

"Okay, he's in the third room on the left. His mom is in there, but I think I can draw her out without her seeing you. But you'll have to move fast."

the woman to go for coffee downstairs, so he had maybe ten minutes.

When he found Mark's room, he walked in on silent feet. The boy was pale, thin, and his spiky punk-rock style hair was brown and stuck out all over his head, giving him a wild look. His eyes were closed, and Zac hoped he wasn't in a deep sleep.

"Mark?"

The eyes opened, looking him over with a dull, disinterested glance. "Go away. Wrong room."

"Mark, I'm Zac. The guy who sent you the letter about Paige."

That got his attention, and his head came up from the pillow. His bottom lip trembled and he asked, "Are you for real, man? Or are you shitting me?"

Again the feeling he was living in a crazy dream came over him, but he had to move forward, tell Mark everything he knew. He pulled an envelope from his pocket, and handed it to the boy.

"I took those photos with my camera a few weeks ago. It's right where she jumped into the water. After that, she started coming to me in a dream. Then I saw her—well, her image for a split second—at the campground. Then, Vicki Sanchez, her friend, held a séance and she talked to us through an Ouija—"

He stopped in mid-babble because there were tears running down Mark's face. He was staring at the photo, and when he looked up there was a pain in his eyes that struck Zac to his core. He had only minutes left, so he started talking again, hoping to get through to the kid so he could get the hell out of this place.

"I know how you feel, Mark. I really do. I lost someone, too. I'm not here to torment you, just to deliver her message. She wants you to be happy and she says what happened to her wasn't your fault." The tears continued, and Zac couldn't think of anything else to say that would make a difference, except, "I'm so sorry, man. But you're young, and you have your whole life ahead of you. Honor her by living the best life you can."

He knew his words were maudlin, but they had the ring of truth. He also felt like a hypocrite, not taking his own advice.

Mark wiped his eyes with the sleeve of his hospital gown, then turned over in the bed to face the wall. As he did so, he threw the photos across the room, scattering them. "You delivered your message. Now go."

The faint ding of the elevator door made Zac's heart leap. As he scrambled to pick up the photos, the click of Mrs. Fitzgill's shoes on the tiles came closer. He made it out the door and slipped around the corner, hoping he hadn't been seen.

He heard Amanda saying goodbye, and he continued down the hall, turning right and then right again, to end up back at the elevator. The nurses he passed at their station gave him the stink eye, but he made it to where Amanda was without incident. They both breathed a sigh of relief as the elevator doors opened.

As they stood inside waiting for the doors to close, a loud female voice called, "Hey, you two, get back here. What the hell do you think you're trying to—"

The door closed, removing the sight of an enraged Mrs. Fitzgill walking toward them.

Amanda let out a guilty-sounding, "Oops."

"Yeah, this is not good. Somebody must have told on me."

The elevator seemed to take forever to move, making him feel claustrophobic. When the doors opened to the first floor, Amanda peeked out, but no one walking by even looked at them. She grabbed his hand and they raced to the car, and as they climbed inside, she asked, "So what did Mark say?"

"He cried when he saw the photos. It was hard to watch. I tried to explain what's been happening with Paige, but he threw the photos on the floor and told me to leave."

"Wow."

"Yeah, and now his Mom's pissed at me, too."

"Maybe she'll send the thugs this time."

He didn't like that thought, especially since Amanda was with him. He doubted they'd do anything to her, Mark's parents couldn't be that bad. Scaring him off was one thing, assaulting a woman was an entirely different matter.

His mood had turned dark. Maybe it was thinking of Gina at the hospital, or Mark's sad eyes. Maybe it was his frustration that he couldn't escape the darkness after so many years. He didn't want it to poison his relationship with Amanda, but would she still love him if she knew the truth?

~*~

Zac told her she should go home, but she sensed he wanted her to stay. He'd been strangely quiet on the drive to his apartment from the hospital. What happened with Mark was upsetting, but his moody reaction seemed out of place. There was something else bothering him, and she watched him as they climbed the stairs to his room. He didn't say a word, but ushered her in with a firm grip on her arm.

As soon as the door latched behind them, he was on her. Kissing her so hard she bent back, almost stumbling. His hands were all over her, his lips moving across her face, her neck. Then Zac picked her up off her feet and carried her to the bed.

They could not shed their clothes fast enough, tossing them to the floor as each piece came off. She giggled a few times at his frantic movements, but was also a teeny bit scared. She'd never seen this side of him. He'd been so gentle before, taking his time. Now it felt like he was going to devour her.

He bit her neck, pinched her nipples. The room was warm and they were sweating already, breath coming fast. His fingers found her center, and she was so wet, excited by his rough attention. He stopped momentarily to roll on a condom, and bent over her, a wild, far-off look in his dark eyes.

Before she could ask what he was thinking, he threw her legs up over his shoulders, and buried himself in her. It was swift, hard, and unexpected. Her breath caught in a gasp, and sharp pain turned to pleasure deep within her. He pulled back, only to slam into her again. His movements were quick, and rough, as though some demonic sexual overlord had taken possession of him. Still, the burning waves of pleasure were building inside, and she tumbled over the edge, crying out her release. She never imagined being taken so completely, so deeply, or that he could scare her and bring her to climax at the same time.

His own release came, and he kept grinding into her, growling like some kind of animal. With one final groan, he collapsed on her, breathing hard. She lay still beneath him, and as the glow of her orgasm faded and sanity returned, she wondered what the hell just happened.

When he finally rolled off her, she turned to him. "Who were you screwing just now? I know it wasn't me."

"What? What are you talking about?"

The furrow of his brow told her he knew something was up, too. Something had driven him to take her like that. She wanted to believe it was just his passion for her, but it felt like something more. "That was really awesome sex, but…you seemed like you weren't really 'with' me just now."

He made a derisive sound, and left to wash up. While he was in the bathroom, she got dressed. His face registered surprise when he saw she was ready to leave. Still naked, he pulled her to him. He kissed her gently, then folded her into a hug. His words were soft, all trace of the caveman she'd just been with were gone. "I'm sorry. I didn't mean to be so rough. Did I hurt you?"

"No. I kind of liked it, but it worried me, too."

"Nothing to worry about. Just too much on my mind lately, I guess."

She watched his face, but his expression didn't give away much. He'd talk when he was ready.

Suddenly thirsty, she went to the kitchen for some water while he dressed. Passing the table, she glanced down at the photos spread out there, and picked one up. "Who's this?"

His voice was soft, hesitant. "That's Gina. My ex."

"From New Jersey? Do you still talk to her?"

She wasn't jealous, really, because he'd never mentioned her. She knew he'd had a hard time when he first moved to Colorado, and maybe it was because of his break up with her.

He sat on the bed, staring into space. "No. She's dead."

There was an uncomfortable silence as the impact of his words hit her. It was not at all what she expected to hear. "Oh. I'm so sorry. I didn't know."

He patted the bed next him, and she sat close, but not touching him. She sensed this was deep territory, but she wanted to know. She wanted more than anything to be able to comfort him.

"We were just outside of Fort Winston, both coming here to attend the college for the first time. It was late at night, and I fell asleep at the wheel. We hit a pole and spun around, then crashed. She died because of me."

There were no words to respond to a statement like that, so she hugged him tight. He held on to her, his body tense. She had always sensed a sadness behind his humor, and now she knew the source of it. "It sounds like it was an accident, Zac. But I'm so sorry for your loss."

He let out a long sigh. "I'm over the worst of it. But I haven't been back home since the funeral, four years ago. Her death sent me into a spiral of debauchery, drugs, and alcohol abuse for a long time. But I pulled out of it, and have been clean ever since."

"Except for the debauchery part. Based on what we just did, I think some of that remains."

A brief smile crossed his lips at her remark, but his eyes still held that far-away look. "But the only way I have been able to handle it is to keep my distance emotionally. That's why I was reluctant to be more than friends with you. I can't really give myself to you, other than physically. I'm damaged."

She knelt in front of him, taking his hands in hers. "You're not damaged, you're just hurting. No one would be able to get over such a thing so easily. I wish you had told me sooner, so I could help you heal."

His eyes went cold, and he stood up, pulling her up with him. "I know you mean well, but I don't need anyone's help. Certainly not their pity."

"Zac, that's not what I meant. I just want to help."

"You better go."

She stood there, unable to think of a way to draw him out of the pity hole he'd fallen into. What had happened to him was horrible, and she wanted to make him forget it, to make his heart whole again. "No, you need me. You're in a dark place, and I can't blame you. But I won't leave you there."

"You need to go. I don't want you here right now."

She stood her ground. "No."

He looked at her as though she'd punched him in the gut. He walked to the kitchen table and with one arm, swiped the photos and letters to the floor. They scattered, and he kicked them toward the trash can by the wall. His voice was hoarse with tension and barely controlled anger. It scared her, but in a different way than his rough lovemaking had.

"There. Is that what you want? I could burn these, or throw them in the trash, but I can't get rid of the memories. Nothing I can ever do will change the fact that she died because of me. Nothing anyone can say will erase that. So you may as well give up trying to fucking save me."

Moving toward him, she fought back a tear. She didn't want him to mistake her tears for pity, because she didn't pity him. They were tears of empathy, and that was different. "Zac...I don't care. I know who you really are. I love you the way you are, the way you've always been."

She hadn't meant to tell him she loved him, it just slipped out. She had to convince him he was not a monster, but a good man, despite his awful past.

He was leaning over the table on his hands, head hung low. "Just go, Amanda. Please."

She left him with a kiss on the cheek and a promise to be there if he needed her. He didn't move, only nodded.

As she drove home, she fought back tears. Just when they had finally connected, the past came back to haunt them.

Then it hit her. Zac had way more in common with Mark Fitzgill than either of them had realized. Both had lost someone they loved, and in their own way, felt responsible for their deaths. It was a fantastic coincidence. Or was it?

19 Warnings

Friday evening, Peggy sat down in her favorite chair in the den with a cold glass of lemonade. It had been a good day. Harriet had called to ask when the next M.A.I.D.s meeting was, being friendly as could be. Then, the Mayor's wife stopped by with a list of possible donors she could contact. And to top it off, Victor had left work early and whisked her upstairs for an afternoon "nap". She had to admit it felt just a bit naughty to be making love while the boys played in the back yard. Afterward, he took the boys out for burgers so she could relax.

To celebrate, she had spiked the lemonade with the last of her vodka, but now Amanda's voice rang in her ears. Her daughter had it wrong, she could quit anytime she wanted. She didn't *need* to drink, she just wanted to.

How about now? Just don't buy another bottle.

But the thought made her nervous. After all, it was just a sip, here and there. Was she really an alcoholic?

No, I'm not like Daddy. He was a drunk.

Memories swirled in her mind of a man who was always there, but she never really knew. She was nothing like him. He was a mean drunk, spewing his anger and insults at everyone. He even hit Mamma, once.

Like I hit Mandy? No, it's not the same thing.

That night he hit Mamma was the last time she saw him. The next morning they left, and she never heard what had happened to him. For all she knew, he was long dead. Mamma remarried years later, and though she liked her stepfather, they were never close. But how could they be, when she had three older brothers ahead of her? No, Peggy didn't begin to really live until she met Victor and left home.

Her drinking was deliberate, controlled, and didn't affect her work or duties. So why did she feel as though she had to hide it?

Her thoughts were interrupted by a knock at the door. Amanda bounded down the stairs from her room to answer it, and let the visitor in. It was Walter, still dressed in his uniform. Peggy could see the Sheriff's car behind him in the driveway.

"What brings you here, Walt? I'm not cooking tonight, but if I'd known you were coming by...."

Her brother removed his hat to reveal thinning red hair, slicked down with sweat. His face had the look of someone about to impart bad news. "No, I can't stay. I just found out something I think you both should know."

She noticed Amanda's eyes shift away to look at the floor as she sank to the sofa. Peggy motioned for Walter to sit, but he declined, shaking his head. "My deputies were called to Powder County hospital yesterday to make a report. It seems a Mrs. Fitzgill wanted to make a complaint about your friend, Zac Daley."

Amanda's skin went pale, the pink in her cheeks fading. Her daughter's hand moved, pulling at the edge of her clothing, a habit she had when she'd been caught doing something she shouldn't. *Mother's intuition strikes again.*

"That's crazy," Amanda finally spoke. "What did she say he's done?"

"She said he came to see her son, Mark, in the hospital without permission. Telling him stories about the ghost of his dead girlfriend, if you can believe that. She also said he'd sent her son a letter about it, which is what set the boy off and caused him to overdose on some pills he'd stolen from her medicine cabinet. To say the woman was upset is an understatement. She wanted to file a restraining order, but there wasn't enough evidence. There was no threat in the letter, and no proof he tried to do anything to physically hurt her son. But she's understandably upset."

Amanda's lip trembled, and she avoided looking at Peggy, keeping her eyes on Walter. "So what will happen now?"

"She's taken the boy home, so maybe she'll cool down, but honestly, I can't say I blame her. She's been though a lot without all this nonsense."

Peggy downed the last of her lemonade. This was too much—now her wonderful day was ruined. She had to get Amanda to see that boy was bad news. If people like the Fitzgill family, who were well known in the community, had a problem with him then she definitely had a problem with him. "See, Mandy? I told you that guy was up to no good. I want you to stay far away from him, is that clear?"

She stood to make her point, glaring at her daughter. Walter shifted from foot to foot, clearly uncomfortable. He cleared his throat after a moment of silence went by, while Peggy stared Amanda down.

"Your mother's right, Mandy. Mrs. Fitzgill was upset with you, too. She said you acted as a decoy, representing your mother's anti-drug group, and taking her for coffee downstairs while your friend slipped into the boy's room. Is that true?"

Amanda stood, her chin raised in defiance. "Yes it is, and I'd do it again. We never meant to hurt anyone, we were only trying to help."

Peggy felt the blood rush to her face. How was she ever going to get this girl under control? Representing my group? What the hell were you thinking, Amanda? Have you no concern for me at all?"

Amanda simply huffed in response, and faced Walter. "What about the two thugs who beat Zac up after he left work at the Cellar bar a few nights ago? I have reason to believe Mark's dad sent them after he intercepted the letter. Who is going to protect him?"

"Well, it's obvious then, that your friend would do well to let the matter drop and keep to himself. And you, young lady, would be better off if you listened to your mother and stayed the heck out of it."

He patted her shoulder, then popped his hat back on his head. Peggy saw him out, and stood watching him leave. Amanda tried to pass her to the stairs, and she grabbed her daughter's arm. "I'm serious, Mandy. This guy is bad news. Now you're getting involved in his shenanigans. I forbid you to ever see him again."

Copper-dark eyes, full of fire, stared back at her. Amanda's mouth twitched, and set in a stubborn line. Then in a steely voice, she said, "And if I continue to see him anyway? What then, Mom?"

Don't you dare taunt me. "Then we'll cut you off."

There was no response as Amanda turned to climb the stairs to her room. She didn't even slam the door.

Peggy hadn't really meant it, she'd never throw her daughter out. But she'd sounded convincing enough, she thought, to get through to the girl. *Tough love.* She'd heard the term somewhere. If that's what she had to use, then by God, she would.

~*~

Night had fallen by the time Amanda got up to wash her face. She'd cried, she'd yelled into her pillow, she threw all of her stuffed animals across the room. Once she'd emptied herself of all the emotions that had warred within her, she grabbed her phone, wrapping the cord around the fingers of one hand while she dialed with the other. Zac would be at work by now, and she had to let him know she'd come to a decision.

"Cellar Bar," she heard him say, his tone clipped.

"Zac, it's me. Sorry to bother you at work."

"It's okay. I'm kinda busy, though. What's up?"

"Well to start, Walter came by and said Mark's mom was royally pissed, wanted a restraining order against you, but there wasn't enough evidence for them to issue one. Then he told my mom I was there at the hospital, too. Let's just say they were not happy."

"Wow. I'm not surprised."

"So, then my mom and I had it out. Again." When he didn't answer, she filled the silence with, "I just can't take it anymore. Living here, I mean. She watches my every move, yet I can't call her out on anything she does. They treat me like a child, and I've had enough of it. Can I stay with you for a while, 'til I can figure something out?"

She held her breath, waiting. When he spoke his hesitant tone made her stomach clench.

"Amanda, I…I don't think it'd be a good idea. I'm giving my notice tonight, and I'll be leaving for New Jersey in a few days. What you said really made me think about how I've been handling things. I have to go back home and face everything there as soon as possible. I've just…put it off for too long. Understand?"

No. No, no no!

She swallowed the lump that had formed in her throat. "Yes. I do understand why you need to go back there. But do you have to leave so soon? We haven't figured out about the ghost girl yet, and my birthday's coming up…"

She was floundering, reaching for anything that might convince him to stay a little longer. It might be selfish of her, but they'd just made love, they had really bonded…hadn't they?

He was distracted then, talking to someone else in the bar. When his attention turned back to her, he said, "Sorry, it's getting busy here. I can meet you somewhere tomorrow and explain, but right now I have to go."

"Goodbye, Zac."

She hung up the phone, and then threw it to the floor, letting out wail of pain. The buzz of the dial tone mocked her, and she reached over to hang it up. There was so much more she wanted to say to him. Like, "No, don't go" and "Take me with you". I need you. I want you.

I love you.

She understood why he needed to leave. She didn't begrudge him that. But after a year of waiting, hoping and wishing, her dream had finally come true, only to be ripped from her the minute she decided she couldn't live without it, without him.

Her face felt puffy again, as tears slid down her cheeks. Staring into space, her eyes lit on her backpack in the corner of the room, and next to it, a small suitcase.

Minutes later, she was down the stairs and out the door, with a suitcase in hand and a backpack slung over her shoulder. If Zac was leaving soon, she was going to spend every last minute with him. And with any luck, she'd either convince him to stay, or to take her with him. As she pulled out of the driveway, she saw her mother standing on the porch with a shocked expression, watching her go.

~*~

Zac wiped down the bar and looked up at the clock. Almost ten. Leah was late again, and he was anxious to let her know what was going on so he could figure out when he could leave town. He didn't want to leave her hanging, being a single mom and all, but he'd made up his mind and wanted to travel as soon as possible. While he still had the nerve. If they could work out a schedule tonight it'd be a relief, and he'd be one step closer to getting back home.

A couple sat down, and he went to take their order. As he was filling their drinks, he looked up to see a familiar face, one had not expected to see again.

Mark Fitzgill's hair still spiked out from his head, looking unwashed. His eyes were dull brown, ringed with dark circles, and his pockmarked skin had a greyish pallor. Bony arms hung limp at his sides, and he leaned over the bar as though afraid to touch it.

Zac came to stand in front of him. "Mark, what're you doing here? You okay?"

"Yeah, I guess…I just wanted to say I'm sorry for being an ass to you yesterday."

His voice was soft, none of the bitter edge it held the day before. Still, he looked like one messed-up kid. "No, don't worry about it. You've been though a lot. But you can't really be in here, man. Twenty one and over, you know."

They never had a bouncer, except nights when there was a band playing. Still, he didn't want or need any more trouble with this kid. Mark looked around, then leaned close. "I know. I'm going, I just wanted to say thanks."

Zac shook the boy's hand, which was thin and unexpectedly cold. "No problem, man, just take care of yourself."

"I will. And do me a favor?"

He couldn't imagine what this guy wanted. Probably wanted drugs, which he was having no part of. "What?"

"Tell Paige I love her, and I miss her every day. And…I hate living without her."

It wasn't what he'd expected to hear, but the kid sounded sincere. He knew how it felt, to live with grief so deep it could hardly be explained. "Sure, Man. I will." He paused, and when Mark didn't say anything, he prompted, "Now go home and get some rest, buddy."

Mark was looking at him, but his eyes held a haunted look, as if the idea of peace was an alien concept. He spoke slowly, like he was figuring out what the words meant for the first time. "Yeah…I'm finally gonna get some rest. Thanks."

His heart ached for the boy, and he watched him leave through the half-open door. A moment later he heard the rumble of a motorcycle come to life. As the sound receded, another face came through the door. A face he knew *he* was going to miss every day. "Amanda. You shouldn't be here."

He'd meant to greet her better than that, but Leah walked in behind her and he didn't want his co-worker to think he was allowing minors to hang out. Though she probably would never guess Amanda was still under twenty-one. His guilt was working overtime tonight.

"I'm so glad to see you, too, Fuzzy. I just need to talk to you, and I promise I won't get in the way."

She sat down on a bar stool at the end of the bar. A group came in, and he spent the next few minutes helping them before he could get to her or tell Leah what was going on. When he finally had a moment, Leah agreed to handle things while he took Amanda outside.

He had every intention of sending her home, but his body and heart had other ideas. Like kissing her all night long, and then some. But there was something else setting him on edge, and it wasn't just her surprise appearance. "I'm glad to see you, but something else just happened. Mark was here a few minutes ago."

"Really? I heard he just got out of the hospital today. What'd he want?"

"He apologized for being a butt when I saw him there. But before he left, he asked me to tell Paige he loved her and missed her, like he believes me now. Which is great, but there was something strange about the way he said it."

"Well, he's been through a lot. And who knows what his parents have been telling him?"

"I know, but it was weird him being out on his motorcycle so soon, and he looked like hell, not much better than he did in the hospital. I told him to go home and get some rest, and he said he would, but…he had an odd tone in his voice."

"You don't think he's going to hurt himself, do you?"

"If that had been obvious, I'd have made him stay until help arrived. But now, I'm not so sure. Anyway, I don't think he's going home at all. Let's go."

Leah was not happy to discover he was leaving the bar that instant, but he explained what was happening, and promised to make it up to her. They were in the VW Beetle and headed up to Horse Tail reservoir in minutes. Amanda insisted on coming, and despite his reluctance, he realized she might be able to help with Mark. He might listen to her, if he couldn't get through to the kid.

As they made their way out of town she asked, "I hate to
say this after what happened earlier, but shouldn't we call the
police and alert them?"

"We should, but only after I get a chance to talk to Mark
alone. You know what'll happen otherwise, they'll just blame
me for stirring him up again. But I don't think anyone else
sees what the real problem is, and I think I can help him if we
get there fast."

"Let me know how I can help."

He didn't answer, just squeezed her hand. It was crazy,
what he was about to do, but something in his gut told him he
had no choice. He put the car in gear and punched the gas. As
he drove through the darkened streets, he glanced in his rearview mirror to see a grayish figure in the backseat, looking
back at him.

And then it was gone.

20 Pursuit

Peggy waited a short time for Victor to get home with the boys, but it was taking too long. They must have gone for ice cream afterwards, and she just couldn't wait any longer. She'd already figured out where her daughter had gone—the Cellar bar. She had simply used Mandy's phone to tell her the last number that had been dialed.

That's where she said he works. Good.

Maybe this time it was Mr. Daley who needed to be set straight, Peggy Bresky-style. Her underage daughter had no business hanging out in a bar, anyway. This had gone way too far, and it had to stop now.

The bar was near the college campus, but on the seedier side of town. When she pulled up, she spotted Mandy's car and marched up to the door of the place, which was propped open to catch the evening breeze. The bar was busy, but there was no sign of Mandy or her friend. She even checked the bathroom, just be sure.

"Ma'am….ma'am?"

She called out, trying to get the bartender's attention, but every seat at the bar was filled with young couples. They were loud and shouting about someone's birthday, as though they had all come in together. The lone bartender, a scrawny girl, was trying to keep up with their demands. This wasn't happening. She had to find her daughter, now.

An idea hit her, so brilliant she would have laughed if she wasn't so worried. She went to her car, and retrieved the item from her backseat. Victor had bought it as a joke, but when she saw it, she had no doubt she'd be able to use it, just not so soon. And she never dreamed it would be because her daughter had run away.

She entered the bar again, and found an empty chair. She stood on the chair, and lifted the bullhorn to her lips. "Your attention please!"

The conversations stopped, and all eyes were on her. "I am Mrs. Bresky and I'm looking for my daughter, Amanda."

Dead silence.

"Red hair, was with the guy who works here, his name is Zac?"

No one said a word, then they started to murmur, some began to laugh. Then the bartender motioned wildly for her to come over to the bar, but she had one more thing to say. "Thank you, that is all. Oh, and don't do drugs."

She climbed down and the bartender met her at the edge of the bar. People moved out of her way now, she noted with satisfaction. She knew the bullhorn would come in handy someday.

"Zac and that redhead just left here a few minutes ago, before this crowd came in," the bartender explained, a note of irritation in her voice. "He said it was some kind of emergency."

"So they must have taken his car. Did he say where they were going?"

"Yeah, up to Horse Tail reservoir. Chasing some kid on a motorcycle. Zac seemed to think the kid was going to hurt himself. Either way, I hope he gets back soon, 'cause I'm swamped."

"Can I use your phone?"

"There's one back by the restrooms. Have at it."

The bartender turned away to help some patrons who were yelling across the bar, and Peggy headed for the phone.

~*~

It was a good thing Zac knew the road to Horse Tail so well. It was pitch black in some spots, with clouds obscuring the moon and no street lights to show the way. He found the old Forestry service road to the abandoned campground, and they bumped along as fast as he could get the Beetle to go over the uneven gravel road.

"What do you think he's going to do?" Amanda asked. She was gripping the door handle but still being jostled as they flew over bumps in the road. He marveled again at how she followed him with no hesitation, even though this was likely to get him into further trouble with Mark's parents, or even with the law.

"I think he's going to jump into the water, like Paige did. You didn't see him in that hospital, did you?"

"Not really, he was asleep when I went in. But from what you told me, I know what happened really messed him up."

"He was in real pain, and what's worse, he blames himself for what happened. I know how that feels."

She placed a hand on his forearm, and only then did he realize how tight his grip was on the steering wheel. He maneuvered around a log half way in the road, and then another. They were losing time. A motorcycle would have flown past all this.

Amanda squeezed his arm reassuringly. "We'll find him. I know we will."

Her words of encouragement helped. He was so busy trying to get to the campground, he had no time to even think of what to say to Mark if he did find him before it was too late. Telling someone in deep grief, 'I know exactly how you feel' was small comfort, no matter how true it was. He'd just have to rely on his instincts when the time came.

Two more hairpin turns and the gravel turned to dirt, so he knew they were getting close. When his headlights bounced off the posts holding the chain that blocked the road, he coasted to a stop. There was no sign of a motorcycle, no sign of anyone, but they got out of the car and stood a moment, listening. He found the path that led to the campground, and he took her hand, hoping they were not too late.

~*~

"I'm coming with you," Peggy informed Walter, standing outside the bar. He'd pulled up in his own car, but two deputies were on the way.

"No, you should go home. I'll handle this and get Amanda home safely, I promise."

They'd been wasting precious time arguing, and she couldn't take it anymore. "I'M GOING WITH YOU," she announced, holding the bullhorn to her lips.

He winced and grabbed the thing from her hands. "Well, get in then. We don't have time for this."

As she settled into the passenger seat, the squad car pulled up, and Walter walked over to give them instructions. Less than a minute later, they were following the squad car, who had red lights blazing and a siren screaming its warning for everyone to get out of their way.

"I don't know what's really going on here, Peggy, but I hope this is the end of it. I had them radio in to have someone call the boy's parents, and we put out an A.P.B. on him."

"I promise you, if I have anything to say about it, this will end tonight. At least for my family."

She settled back, more worried about Mandy than ever. What if this was just some excuse so Zac could get out of work? What if he was meeting Mark to give him more drugs? She didn't trust that guy as far as she could throw him, no matter what her daughter said.

She knew love made you do stupid things.

She also knew she'd forgive her daughter, if she could just hold her again and know she was safe. As they sped to the edge of town, she saw the black shape of the hills surrounding the reservoir looming in the distance. Mandy was up there, somewhere, and she could not get to her fast enough.

Walter's CB radio was buzzing with static, distracting her. He was monitoring the conversations between the deputies and the sheriff's station and it had just been confirmed that Mark's parents had been reached and informed of the situation. In her worry over Mandy's safety, she hadn't thought much about the boy, or his parents.

"Walt, do you think that Fitzgill kid is really going to hurt himself? Maybe he's back on the dope."

"It's possible. His mother told me he'd been severely depressed since the incident last year, when his girlfriend died. Could be he's going to re-visit the scene where it happened, so that's where we're headed now."

"Poor kid. But none of it would have happened if they hadn't had access to drugs. Such a shame."

Walter maneuvered around a turn, the tires squealing. He spoke casually, as though they were sitting in the backyard, not speeding down the road, chasing a wayward teenager. "We don't really know that, Peggy. When all that happened at the hospital, I took a look at the file on the case. All we know is what the boy told us. The girl may have had other problems that caused her to do what she did. We'll never know."

"Well, all I know is, when it comes to drugs, trouble always follows."

"That's true, but you know what? The bulk of our domestic disturbance calls, and many of the accidents on the roads, are alcohol-related. It causes much more tragedy than illegal drugs do, if you want to know the truth. It tears families apart, and causes more deaths each year."

"Interesting."

"But at least there are some services for alcoholics, though. We've got two groups in town dedicated to twelve-step programs and such. But we definitely need help for the drug addicts, too."

"You know that's why I started my group, to help people."

Peggy didn't say anything else, just sat staring at the flash of the red lights and listening to the blare of the siren. Did she really want to know the truth?

What Walter hadn't said made as much impact on her as his words did. *Alcoholics just like our father, and what he did to our family.*

Her father hadn't set a good example for any of them. So what kind of an example had she been setting for her children? She'd been telling herself it was not a problem, because no one else knew about her drinking. But now that Mandy knew, things were different.

She promised herself once this mess got straightened out tonight, and she knew Mandy was safe, there would be some changes made. Her children were too precious to her to let them down.

21   Truths

They were running through the dark, tripping over branches and ruts in the path. The campground looked different at night than she remembered, and Amanda was glad she wore her sneakers that night instead of flip-flops. Zac was zigzagging around bushes and she kept up, watching his back and listening for any sound other than their feet hitting the dirt.

As they came upon the clearing near the cliff overlooking the lake, he stopped. As she caught up, she saw the motorcycle laying on its side in the dirt. A figure was standing at the edge of the cliff and it turned to face them, arms out in a "stop" motion.

"Don't come any closer. I mean it," Mark yelled, holding up one hand in a threatening stance.

"What's he got?" she whispered, hoping it wasn't a gun.

"Looks like a knife."

Zac's voice was calm, though he was still breathing heavily from their sprint to the campground. He held up his hands in a friendly gesture, and took a step forward. "Mark, I just want to talk. Put down the knife, buddy."

"I'm not your buddy. Stay right there." He held up the knife, and backed closer to the edge.

Amanda watched as Zac took another step, then stopped. He'd must have heard it, too—the wail of a police car's siren echoing up the mountain. She looked in the direction of the sound to see headlights bouncing off the rocks below. "Oh crap. Cavalry's coming."

Zac swore under his breath, and took another step. "Mark, I'm coming over. I just want to talk before anyone else gets here, okay? Then we'll leave you alone."

The boy lowered his arm a few inches, but kept the knife pointed out. As Zac got closer, Mark didn't move, but

watched with wary eyes. When Zac stopped moving, Amanda
had also crept close enough to hear every word he said.

"Mark, what are you doing, man? When you came to the
bar earlier you seemed like you had made peace with things."
His casual tone seemed to soften the boy's defenses. The
hand holding the knife dropped to his side, and Mark's voice
was little more than a sob. "I'll never have peace. How can I?
How can I when it's my fault she's dead?"

The blare of a siren became suddenly loud and then died
down in long wail, followed by the sound of car doors slamming. There was a rustling of bushes and the pounding of feet
on dirt, and a few moments later two sheriff's deputies came
into view with guns pointed at them. They were followed by
a larger man and a woman, who hung back in the darkness of
the bushes.

"Don't shoot," Amanda called, her hands up. "Just wait,
he needs to talk to the boy, to save him."

"Out of our way, Ma'am, get back there where it's safe,"
one of the deputies said, as he passed her. She recognized the
burly form of her uncle, and ran to him.

"Walter, please? Make them stop. He only has a knife, no
guns. And Zac can save him, help him. I know he can."

To her relief, Walter conceded. "Stop your advance. Give
them a moment."

"Thank you," she breathed, and ran to stand a few feet
away from Zac. The others stood a foot or so behind her, and
she knew they could all hear the exchange.

Mark had raised the knife again when the officers appeared. He was now perilously close to the edge, looking over
his shoulder at the lake below.

"Listen to me, and forget about them," Zac said, his voice
commanding, yet calm as the inky black night around them.
"Just a few years ago, I was driving my car south of town and
I fell asleep at the wheel. We spun around and crashed into a
pole. I was banged up, but my girlfriend, Gina...well, she
died. So I do know what you're feeling, man. I really do. It

hurts like hell, it makes you hate yourself. You wish it was you that died, instead of her."

Something twisted in Amanda's gut. She had no idea the kind of guilt Zac had been living with. She could not imagine what she'd do, being responsible for something bad happening to the ones she loved. She understood now why Zac had kept her away from his heart for so long.

Mark's head was down, and he was crying. He still held the knife in his hand, but was listening to Zac, who kept going, on a mission to save the boy, and maybe even himself. "But you got lucky, Mark. Paige came to me, to give her message to you. She loves you, she wants you to live. She forgives you."

At that, the boy broke down completely, sobbing loudly. Then the knife in his hand came up, and he pointed it at his own heart, the tip touching his shirt. Gasps came from the men, and the woman in the shadows said, "Oh, no. Please don't."

She recognized the voice, and looked to see her mother standing behind Walter. *Oh, crap, Mom?* But her eyes returned to see what Mark would do next.

In a shaky voice, the boy spoke. "But I can't forgive myself. I don't know how. We…we were graduating. We came up here to celebrate, and were gonna do it for the first time."

His words came out in a rush now, voice cracking with emotion. "We were virgins. I thought maybe we wouldn't be so nervous if we smoked some pot first, that's all. I never thought it would be so strong. It made me sick, but she got all dizzy and paranoid. She tried to run away, she was freaking out, and she…went over."

Zac was only a foot away now, close enough to touch Mark. He lifted a hand, reaching out to take the knife. "No one blames you, Mark. You have a chance to make it right, though. Do you know how?"

His next word was a hoarse whisper. "How?"

"By living the life she couldn't have. By making her proud of you, becoming the best person you can be. By helping others who are in need. If you hurt yourself with drugs and alcohol, or you end it all, you are not honoring her, and her death will have been in vain."

The knife dropped to the ground, and Mark fell to his knees. 'I'm so sorry Paige. I really loved you. I'm sorry."

Zac knelt down, his arm around the boy. "It's okay, buddy. I'll help you. I went through it, and I can help you get through it. And believe me, you'll find yourself again. And you'll find love again, I promise."

Tears fell down Amanda's face and she wiped them away. She fell more in love with her man than ever, and knew that even if he left her tomorrow, she was honored to have known the true person he was.

The deputies rushed in and one guided Mark away, while the other placed the knife in a plastic bag. Walter came over, followed by her mother, and Amanda stiffened, waiting for the lectures. To her amazement, Peggy embraced Zac in a bear hug.

"You handled that boy magnificently, young man. My heart just about stopped, but you had the situation under control. Bless you." She turned to her daughter, and tackled her with a hug, too. "I'm still not happy with you, Mandy. But I guess it was all for a good cause."

"Yes, Mom. I've been trying to tell you to just trust me. But it was all worth it for you to see Zac the same way I do. He's awesome."

"Let's not get carried away, now," Zac said. "I just did what I had to do, told him what he needed to hear."

Peggy was still holding on to Amanda's arm, as though she would never let go. She was also looking at Zac in a way Amanda had never seen—with admiration. When she spoke, her tone was a mixture of awe and conviction.

"Well, it was what I needed to hear, too. I'm sorry I underestimated you all this time. I suppose I got so carried away with figuring out how to prevent drug addiction, I forgot about helping those who have succumbed. It's not always as easy as just saying, 'no', is it?"

"No, Ma'am. Everyone has their own reasons, their own tragedies to deal with. But I'm living proof that you can start over again."

Walter slapped Zac on the back, leading them all away from the campground. "That was a good job, son. I think Mrs. Fitzgill will calm down a bit, when her son is home safe. Anyway, I'll put in a good word for you."

Once they were back at the cars, Walter strapped Mark's motorcycle into his trunk, and the deputies led the way down the mountain in the squad car. It was a much more subdued ride on the way back than the frantic race up had been. They were drained and tired, and Amanda found she didn't have much to say until they neared the bar.

"Zac, I never had the chance to tell you what I came to say."

"Which was?"

Her earlier emotions had flown in the face of a larger crisis, but she knew what she had to do. "I know why you have to leave, and it's okay. I understand. But I want to spend every minute with you until you go. You said you would never push me away again."

They were turning into the Cellar bar parking lot. She had waited too long.

"I did say that, didn't I? Well, I can't go back on my word."

Her heart leapt. "You mean that? I can stay over at your place until you leave?"

"Yes. And you know what else?"

Her heart was pounding annoyingly hard now. "What?"

"I want you to go to New Jersey with me."

"For real? For how long?"

He parked the car, then took her hand. "I'd say a few weeks. We'll be back long before school starts again. I want you to meet my family."

She threw her arms around his neck, and smothered his bushy beard with kisses. She was so ecstatic, she ignored her mother's tapping on the car window.

~*~

It was nearly two a.m. when they finally closed the bar. Leah had been understanding once Zac told her what went down, but she was not happy to hear he was leaving town. He didn't say anything about when he'd return, even though he'd decided to stay in Fort Winston. Keeping his options open seemed right, and Leah mentioned Mr. Drake, the owner of the bar, would likely welcome him back if he ever needed a job.

It had been a crazy night. Hell, a crazy week. But now he was going home to Amanda, who was warming his bed at the moment. He'd given her the key to his room, and she looked at him as though it was encrusted with diamonds. Even more surprising, her mother only grimaced when Amanda informed her she would be home in the morning. He'd expected fireworks over that, but apparently Mrs. Bresky really had altered her opinion of him.

What he said to Mark on that cliff was true, and as he said the words, it became clear to him he should follow his own advice. He needed to honor Gina's memory, not hide from it. He'd beaten his addictions to drugs and alcohol, but he still hadn't opened his heart. Giving back to others was a big part of that, and so was being able to accept love.

And love was all Amanda had ever wanted from him.

Fatigue was setting in as he climbed the stairs to his door, but his mind was still wired. The adrenaline he'd felt while talking to Mark on that ledge had worn off, but he wasn't sleepy yet. He hoped Amanda wasn't, either.

She answered his knock at the door, dressed in an over-sized tee shirt and panties—nothing else. He took her in his arms and devoured her mouth in a long, slow kiss. Pulling back, he looked at her, thinking how lovely she looked, even without makeup. Her pink, sun-kissed cheeks were peppered with freckles, and her coppery-red locks had also been struck with highlights from the sun.

"I can't believe I'm going to wake up next to you in the morning. I haven't spent the whole night with anyone since…"

"Shhh…" She placed her fingers over his mouth. "There's nowhere else I'd rather be than here with you, Fuzzy. You were such a hero tonight. It made me realize, you always have been. You're just that kind of guy."

He laughed. "I'm just a regular guy, trying to do the right thing. Man, I wish everyone could see me the way you do. No, wait. I'd probably get a big head."

"At least Mom's changed her mind about you. Now we can be together, do whatever we want."

He nuzzled her neck, loving the softness of her skin. "Hmmm…whatever we want? I know what I want right now…"

He reached down to stroke her thigh, trailing his fingers upward, until he reached her panties. Her giggle turned into a gasp as he stroked her, enjoying the feel of the silky material and the dampness of her arousal. He slipped a finger inside to find her slick, hot and ready. She squirmed and pressed against his hand, a whimper escaping her lips.

Her hand had strayed to the bulge in his jeans, rubbing back and forth, causing him to become painfully hard. He wanted her more each time he took her, with a frantic passion that bordered on addiction. But it was the type of addiction he never wanted to quit.

Pulling away, he struggled to shed his clothes as her tee-shirt and panties fell to the floor. He kissed her hard, then walked over to his nightstand. He rolled on a condom, then led her to a chair in the kitchen. He sat down, and she needed no prompting. She eased down onto his shaft with a sigh, and he closed his eyes as the sharp pleasure overtook him.

His hands grabbed her hips, but she took control. Rotating, moving back and forth, up and down, he let her move how she wanted. He had to concentrate on keeping control of himself, not wanting it to end too soon. It was difficult, feeling her so hot and wet, wrapped tight around him, but he held on. She rocked in a rhythm, moaning and crying out as her orgasm built, throwing her head back as she shuddered through it. When her cries subsided, he let go, pushing hard into her, crying out his own release. Her head lay on his shoulder, and they sat for a long time just holding on, the burning need that bound them turning into a warm glow.

Later, as they lay in the dark, he held her close. He still couldn't sleep, thinking of the events of the night. Was it truly over? Would Mark Fitzgill finally find peace? He hoped so. He felt a glimmer of peace within his own soul, something he hadn't dared to feel in years.

He opened his eyes, staring into the dark. The sensation of being watched had come again, but his eyes were heavy with fatigue. As he closed them, he heard a whisper.

"Thank you."

Amanda turned to him, murmuring, "What'd you say?"

But he hadn't spoken. "Nothing. Go to sleep, Babe."

He waited a moment, until her breathing was deep. To the empty room, he whispered, "Thank *you*."

22   Farewells

Saturday morning, Peggy kept busy cleaning house. She didn't want to think about where her daughter was, so the distraction of scrubbing floors and dusting helped. She'd made the decision the night before to let Amanda do what she felt was right, and though she didn't agree, it was a small step forward in letting go of her baby girl.

She's a woman now, and I have to trust her.

They had talked many times about the consequences of sex, about birth control. Though she would prefer her daughter to remain a virgin until marriage, she wasn't naïve enough to believe she could force the issue. Other parents had worse problems with their kids than Mandy had given her so far, and that was a blessing.

It was also a relief to discover Zac Daley was not as bad as she believed, and he was a man of integrity and compassion. The young man had been through so much in his life, and she could respect him for that. The reason she took on the cause of preventing illegal drug use was to help young people, and it made her cringe when she realized her own behavior had crossed the line from helping to causing trouble. No real harm was done in the end, and for that she was grateful.

An hour later, the first floor was sparkling clean, and would remain that way as long as she could keep the boys outside. They were swimming in the neighbor's pool and wouldn't be back until suppertime, so she decided to tackle the upstairs next. In her bedroom, the repetition of movement while working allowed her mind to wander, and Walter's words as they raced up the mountain to the reservoir came to mind. She had been surprised to learn that alcohol was bigger problem in the county than illegal drugs had ever been.

Her family was the most important thing in the world to her, certainly more important than alcohol. It took witnessing a near-suicide to make her realize how precious they were to her. What if one of her sons had been in Mark's shoes? His parents were upstanding citizens, and provided a good home, yet nothing could prevent what happened. Children ultimately make their own choices.

"But I won't set a bad example. I'm not like my father," she said out loud, her conviction clear. She walked to the closet and found the flask, wrapped in a scarf and hidden behind a pair of boots. She tossed it, scarf and all, in the wastebasket. That phase of her life was over.

But as she'd told Zac, it wasn't as easy as just saying it was over. She needed help and support, just as her nephew, Walt's son Jeffrey, had. It was the incident which had started her on this path, and now she realized she had to take the next step, if she was going to set an example for her family and the community. With a trembling hand, she sat on the edge of the bed, picked up the phone and dialed her brother's number.

"Walt, it's Peg. I need the number of that twelve-step support group you mentioned...no, it's not for a friend...it's for me."

They talked for a while, and she was surprised at how non-judgmental Walter was. He promised to help in any way he could, because, as he said, "That's what families do." Her father's horrible legacy had been broken, and somehow that satisfied her in a deep, untouched part of her soul. She realized then how much strength it took to admit you needed help.

The sense of relief she felt at taking her leap of faith faded a bit as she passed Mandy's open door. The pink and purple décor seemed juvenile, as did the rock star posters on the wall, and the stuffed animals in every corner. She preferred her friends call her Amanda now, and perhaps it was time her family did, too. She would be twenty-one soon, of legal age. An adult, with all the rights and responsibilities that entailed.

That was the natural progression of life, and Peggy realized she was looking forward to the next phase, not dreading it. She closed her daughter's bedroom door with a sad smile.

~*~

Only a week had passed since the night at Horse Tail reservoir, but to Amanda it seemed a world away. She wanted to pinch herself to be sure she wasn't dreaming. But no, she really was traveling down the highway out of Fort Winston, on her first road trip, and best of all, she was with the man she loved.

Her parents had fussed and lectured, but it made her feel good to know they cared. Her dad had made sure the VW Beetle was road ready, helping Zac with a tune up and oil change. He even helped them pack the car, though there wasn't room for much. Her mom had packed them a basket of food, enough to sustain them for at least two states.

"They were acting like I was leaving home for good, not for a few weeks," she laughed as they turned on to the highway that stretched south to Denver. "I thought we were never going to get away."

"Just wait until you see how my family acts when we try to leave New Jersey."

She laughed, but the thought of meeting his family made her queasy. They probably still mourned his last girlfriend, and it was a tough position to be in, being compared to a ghost. But he'd told her to just be herself, and they would accept her in time. She hoped so, and Peggy's acceptance of him was nothing short of a miracle, so anything was possible.

They were barely to the next town, when he pulled over at the side of the road. There was no gas station or stores nearby, so she looked over at him, feeling puzzled. "Why are we stopping here?"

He shut off the engine, and sat staring at the empty field on the other side of the road. "This is where it happened."

He got out, and stood looking at the site. All she saw was a telephone pole, wire fencing and cows grazing in the distance. She watched him walk across the road before deciding to follow. They stood there in silence, the prairie wind rustling the grass in a forlorn song. Occasional cars whizzed by, with no reason to stop on this desolate section of highway.

"I haven't been back here, but I needed to stop," he said, his voice quiet, almost reverent.

"I understand."

There wasn't much she could say, so she leaned up against him, holding onto his arm. He reached in his pocket and pulled out a rock. It was large, about palm-sized, smooth and round. He turned it over in his hand, explaining.

"She gave me this one day at the beach, on the Jersey Shore. She carved our initials in it, see?"

Amanda nodded, smiling. It was important to him, this memento. She liked that he had a sentimental side.

He leaned down, and pulled a handful of grass out, burying the rock. Tamping the grass and dirt over it, he stood. "This is where she died. It belongs here, with her."

Tears threatened, but she blinked them back. It touched her heart to know how deeply he could feel. There was a time where she believed he was unable to feel the way she did, to love. But she knew better now, and stood silent, happy to be there for him.

His voice held a note of relief when he spoke. "Let's go. I promise to get you to New Jersey and back, safe and sound."

"I had no doubt, Fuzzy. You know I'd follow you anywhere."

Holding hands, they crossed the road and got back in the car, heading toward their future.

Epilogue

Later that summer

"Hey, look what I brought."

Zac couldn't resist teasing Amanda, and held up the vintage camera to his face. He snapped a picture as she stuck out her tongue at him.

"Well, I guess you have to use something to record my birthday party. I just hope it's ghost-free this time."

"Yeah, me too."

He followed her out of the house and into the backyard, which was teeming with people. This was her parent's gift for her twenty-first birthday—a party complete with catered food and a band. Granted, they were playing soft-pop hits, but people were dancing and having a good time. There were more of her parent's friends there than any of theirs, but he was beginning to feel more comfortable around Peggy and her entourage. Once in a while someone gave him the side-eye, but for the most part they accepted him as Peggy's daughter's boyfriend, just as he was.

Amanda stopped in front of the table that held the food, admiring the large bouquet of flowers that had been placed in the center. The flowers had long, elegant stalks with several blossoms, ranging from small to larger sizes they climbed the stalk. Yellow, peach and pink, they had been expertly arranged in a decorative vase. As she reached out to touch one, a woman about her mother's age appeared at her elbow.

"Those are gladiolas," she explained. "They're the August birth flower."

Zac stood aside as Amanda embraced the woman. "Thanks, Harriet. I should have known it was you who brought them. They're beautiful."

She introduced her then to Zac, noting, "She's a florist. Her shop is downtown."

He shook the woman's hand, still holding the vintage camera. Harriet's eyes went wide and she gasped, and he wondered what he'd done wrong.

"That camera, is it yours? Where did you get it?"

"Yes. She gave it to me a few months ago."

He looked at Amanda, who added, "I got it at a pawn shop downtown."

"May I see it?"

He nodded, handing the camera over to Harriet. She looked at the thing as though she recognized it, turning it over in her hands, inspecting it. Finally, she handed it back to him, asking, "Did it come with a case?"

"Yes. It was in amazing shape considering how old it was."

She gave him an odd look. "I bet there were initials carved in the case, right? If so, that was my mother's camera."

"Yeah, I saw some initials, 'R.R.'".

Harriet seemed pleased, but there was a touch of sadness around her eyes. "Rita Rothmeyer. Before she died, she gave it to my niece, Paige, who was only about ten then. I guess when Paige got older she decided to pawn it. What a shame."

There was an awkward silence as his brain tried to comprehend what the woman had just said. Amanda was looking from Harriet to him, and back again, her mouth open in surprise. He looked the camera over again, unable to believe the connection. "So Paige owned this camera? I'll be a son of a..."

He shut his mouth before he could offend the woman. A chill ran up his neck, though the August weather was warm, and unusually humid. He looked at Amanda and asked a silent question, in the way that couples do. She raised a brow and inclined her head, almost imperceptibly. He offered the camera to Harriet.

"Oh, no, I didn't mean...I would never..."she stammered, and Amanda placed a hand on her arm.

"It belongs in your family. Please, take it."

A tear formed at the corner of Harriet's eye, and she wiped it away with the back of her hand. "I tell you what. You take some photos of the flowers that I can use later at the shop. That way, we all can enjoy it."

Then she hugged them both, and wandered over to where Peggy and some other women were gathered.

"What just happened?" Amanda asked, taking his arm.

"Hell if I know. Just promise me this—no more surprises."

She laughed. "Yeah. I'll keep that in mind."

"You'd better." He looked around, started taking photos of the table, the flowers, the guests. She watched, in between hugs and well-wishes from people as they passed.

Later, he leaned over to whisper in her ear. "The real party is tonight, at the Cellar. You have to have at least one drink to celebrate being legal."

She grinned wickedly. "You don't have to get me tipsy to get me into bed, you know."

"I know, it doesn't take much at all, and not even a bed. A chair, a table, the floor…"

She punched his arm. "Hey, isn't that your friend Sarah?"

Her finger pointed to the petite brown-haired woman who'd just come around the corner of the house, looking lost. She was one of the few friends he'd invited, having lost touch with so many, who had all moved on after graduation.

He called to her, and they met her near the food table. After getting drinks, they sat on a blanket under a big oak tree, just as the band started up their rendition of a popular love song.

"Dang," Sarah said. "That's a good song, but you know, love isn't always enough to keep two people together."

Zac snapped some photos of the band, then turned the camera on Sarah and Amanda. "Trouble in paradise, McKenn?"

His old friend always had an expressive face, and her pain showed clearly now. Her voice quieted and she looked away. "Let's just say that life blew up in my face lately. Nothing has gone the way I was hoping."

"Sorry to hear that. I was wondering why Chris wasn't here with you."

Sarah lifted her cup in salute. "That's a story for another day, my friend. I'm just glad I got to see you before I left town. I'm moving back home to Denver in a few days. Anyway, today is for the Birthday Girl. Happy Birthday, Amanda!"

A few people in the crowd overheard her, and a round-robin of birthday wishes began. Soon the crowd was on its feet, and the band stopped in mid-song to wish Amanda a happy birthday. She blushed, but Zac knew she loved the attention. He also knew she deserved it, for being the kind of person she was. Even his family, not the friendliest group to outsiders, had become smitten with her.

Amanda's parents stood nearby, beaming with pride. To his surprise, her mother had turned into one of his biggest supporters, even using her influence to help him get a position with the Office of Tourism and Development. His life had fallen into place, and this was where he belonged.

His heart swelled, and he put his arm around Amanda, claiming her as his own for the whole world to see. He knew deep in his soul, that he could handle whatever surprises life threw his way, as long as she was by his side.

THE END

About the Author

A lifelong entrepreneur, Renee Regent spent most of her life writing for business. But she never lost her love of writing stories, especially romance, science fiction, and fantasy. She's always been fascinated with the science of how the universe works, but equally entranced by the unexplained. Being an incurable romantic, she now writes stories about the power of love, with a supernatural twist. Her stories feature psychics, witches, ghosts and ordinary people who do extraordinary things.

Renee, a California native, lives in Atlanta with her husband, three cats and four turtles. When not working or writing, she can be found sitting on her deck enjoying nature. Wine may or may not be involved....

A member of Georgia Romance Writers and the Georgia Writer's Association, Renee also loves blogging and sharing her ideas on the business side of being an author, trends in fiction, and tips she has learned in her writing journey.

Now available - Unexplained (Higher Elevation Series Book One)

Coming soon - Undeniable (Higher Elevation Series Book Three) January 2017

Thank you for reading. Honest reviews are always appreciated.

If you would like more information, stop by my website at http://reneeregent.com for news on upcoming releases, blog posts, special events, social media links, and to sign up for my newsletter.

Made in the USA
Charleston, SC
27 November 2016